DRAGONSTONE DANCE

LINDA WINSTEAD JONES

Dragonstone Dance, Copyright 2017 by
Linda Winstead Jones.
Print Edition, 2017

ISBN-13: 978-1544889375
ISBN-10: 1544889372

Cover design by Elizabeth Wallace
http://designwithin.carbonmade.com/

Print formatting by A Thirsty Mind Book Design
http://www.athirstymind.com/

CHAPTER ONE

The twentieth year of the reign of Emperor Nechtyn Jahn Calcus Sadwyn Beckyt

Demons came and demons went. Linara, sitting with her back to the wall, watched the crowd in the tavern. Lately, more demons — half demons like her — had come. The war was hurtling toward an end and they all felt it. A few had run away from the fight, but more wanted to be a part of it.

None of them could feel what the final outcome would be, and still they came.

No men were in the tavern tonight. While they had joined the demon side of the fight, they were naturally nervous when such a large crowd gathered together. The energy was like lightning. Even a human could feel it.

A newcomer, a pretty girl of twenty years — as they all were — approached Linara with a smug smile. A nervous redhead trailed behind her. "So you are the great Ksana," the new girl said.

"I prefer to be called Linara." Neither her voice nor her face revealed any emotion. To be honest, she preferred not to be called at all, not by her sisters or the soldiers who had aligned themselves with this dark side, but it was impossible to be invisible in such a crowded place.

The newly arrived demon tossed a glance over her shoulder to look at her companion. "She does not look at all powerful."

Linara stood slowly. All the women in her vicinity instinctively backed away. She had found no extraordinary powers, nothing to live up to her reputation as the first born and most powerful. But they did not know with certainty what she could do. Her reputation, as well as her close relationship with Stasio, the dark wizard who commanded them all, protected her.

Without a word, Linara made her way through the crowd. It parted for her.

What would they do if they knew the only power she'd discovered within herself was a bit of telepathy?

She stepped into the cool night and rounded the noisy building. Laughter and voices were muted, and for that she was thankful.

Alone at last, Linara stood well back from the tavern, looking over the rooftop and toward the mountains in the distance. The full moon was just a few days past, and generous moonlight lit the alternating harsh stone and lush green of the mountaintop. It was a soothing sight, promising a kind of paradise close and yet not close enough. Each night for the past year, since she'd come to this village in the Northern Province of Columbyana, she'd stepped outside soon after dark and waited. Some nights she only had to wait minutes. Other nights she waited for hours.

She didn't mind waiting; she had all the time in the world.

Linara Varden, daughter of a demon and adopted daughter of Sophie and Kane Varden, was a small part of a powerful army that had been four years in the making. A year ago, this village had been deemed an appropriate plot of land to claim as their own. It was isolated, well away from the larger towns and the capital city of Arthes. The former inhabitants had fled, unable to stand against the dangerous invaders.

Stasio — the dark wizard who had appointed himself leader of the daughters of the Isen Demon — wanted control of Columbyana handed to the half-demons, and to himself as their proxy, of course. He believed that by virtue of their power alone, they deserved it. The emperor, his soldiers, and his people thought otherwise. The emperor's forces hadn't yet amassed their full might on this village. Linara knew it wouldn't be long. She felt it.

There were moments, days even, when she considered leaving this place for good. Her mother — the woman who had adopted her soon after birth — would welcome her home. Of that, she had no doubt. At the thought of Sophie Fyne Varden, Linara touched the small pink stone that hung around her neck. She caressed the stone, gave thanks for it, and cursed it at the same time. The amulet, blessed by Sophie and her sisters, made Linara different from others of her kind. It had thus far kept her from becoming a killer who drained lives to feed her own.

She suspected the amulet which made it possible for her to survive without killing also muted any powers she might possess. And still, she did not remove it. Not yet.

Linara had always felt apart from her demon sisters, and the reason was no secret. She was both demon and beloved daughter. She hated and she loved.

On this night, she didn't have to wait long for that which she most desired to see. Above the eastward mountain peak, far in the distance, it appeared. There wasn't much more than a speck at first, but then a flickering tendril of flame turned into an impressive inferno that illuminated, too briefly, the dragon who had spit that fire into the night sky.

One born, one hatched, one created. Fourteen years ago, it had been prophesied that those three would be required to defeat the daughters of the Isen Demon.

Stasio claimed that the dragon was the "one hatched." While there were other shifters who had the ability to fly, they had been born. They were humans who could take a form not their own, not a true beast of the air. If the humans ever brought the dragon to their side of this war, the effects would be devastating. Linara and her sisters were hard to kill, but they could — and did — die. Beheading or fire, those were certain methods of death, even for a half-demon. A dragon's flame would do nicely, she imagined.

Stasio also said General Merin's daughter was the one born. That made no sense to Linara, though she did accept it as truth. She'd learned not to disregard Stasio's knowledge and wishes. The wizard had impressive powers. Still, she could not be afraid of a human child. Who would be?

Not even Stasio knew who or what the one created might be.

As if he had known she was thinking of him — and perhaps he had — Stasio rounded the building, his eyes on her. He was old enough to be her father, but there was nothing fatherly about him. She knew what a real father was like. Kane Varden had shown her, all the days of her life. Dark haired with even features and a slender body, the wizard might be viewed as ordinary enough if not for his eyes, which were dark as a moonless night and swimming with evil. He possessed magic, as Sophie had, but his magic was dark. Stasio had the power to look into Linara's head, to rummage through her thoughts, to visit her in her dreams and in her waking hours.

More than anything, he wished for her to find and embrace whatever demonic powers she possessed. He insisted they were within her, waiting to be awakened and released. He had been oddly patient with her. What did he know that he had not told her?

The amulet she wore made it possible for Linara to survive without taking the lives of others, but it did nothing to take away the poison. She would never lie with a man, never have a child, never know what it was like to love as her parents had. Never.

So why did she pretend that she was different from the others?

Looking squarely at Stasio, she caressed the amulet, held on tight, and then yanked hard. The thin chain bit into her neck and then snapped. Without a second thought, she tossed it away into the brush at the edge of this cursed village.

"I'm ready to play my part."

The relief on Stasio's face was evident. "I knew you would feel it when the time was right."

A part of her, a small part, wanted to rush into the dark brush and find the stone she'd tossed away so impulsively. Unless she retrieved the amulet and returned it to its place around her neck, she would soon need to kill to survive. Perhaps tomorrow the hunger would come. Perhaps it would not come for a week or even a month. The Ksana demons were all different in that regard, and she did not know what her requirements would be.

"You will kill the dragon," Stasio said. "That is your destiny. I have seen it in my dreams."

Linara had the fleeting thought that it would be wrong to kill such a magnificent creature. Were there more of its kind in the world, or was it the only one? She had no way of knowing, but at the very least it was a rare creature. She had never seen or heard of another.

When she stood here and watched the dragon each night, she was not only studying flight and flame patterns and trying to discern which mountain the beast called home, she was admiring the strength and beauty of him. Her. It. Who could know?

Stasio reached out and grabbed her upper arm, holding on too tight. Linara glared at that hand with disdain, then looked up and into those evil eyes. He might try to scare her, but she knew no fear. She never had.

"I did not give you permission to touch me, wizard."

He didn't drop his hand as he should've. "I did not give you permission to look upon the dragon with anything other than ill intent."

She could block Stasio from her mind, but it had taken years of practice and still required effort. Whether he was near or far, he slipped in too easily as if he belonged there, as if he had a right to pry. Linara did not block him now. Instead, she thought of kissing him, of laying her mouth on his and draining the life from him. She thought of holding him to her until there was nothing left. Nothing but skin and bones and an empty pile of clothing. She made a point to think of the black glove that touched her laying atop the gray clothing he now wore.

He wanted her to embrace her demon side. Why not show it to him?

He released her as if he had been burned. It was difficult to tell in this light, but she was almost positive he paled.

Stasio had lured her from home, and then he had nurtured the monster in her. He did not wish to be her first victim.

"You've always said slaying the dragon was my destiny, but you have never said how I might accomplish such a task. How do you expect me to kill such a beast?"

"You will find a way," he said.

"Do you expect me to walk into those mountains without a plan?" Without an army?

"I do. I can send a hired swordsman with you, if you'd like. You might have need of one before you reach your destination."

Not for his sword, she realized, but for his essence. Someone to serve as her first victim.

"I can only spare one," Stasio added. "The emperor's army grows closer."

It was entirely possible — no, it was almost certain — that she had cousins in that army. Perhaps even a brother or a nephew. None of them would be blood relatives, of course. Only her demon sisters could be considered related by blood. Still, for sixteen of her twenty years, the children and grandchildren of the Fyne sisters had been her family.

Linara accepted who she was; she would learn to embrace her true nature, but if she came face to face with someone she had once considered family...

They were not her family, not anymore.

"I'll go alone, and I leave tonight." Again, she considered taking a detour through the brush to collect her amulet, but she did not.

The witch who had taken her in as a baby might've loved her as a child, but no one who embraced light and goodness and life could truly love the demon inside her. Yes, it was past time to put Linara behind her and become Ksana.

It was past time to kill the dragon.

Many women were considered fully grown at thirteen. Thirteen *and a half,* to be precise. In a couple of years, she might legally marry, not that she had any intention of doing so. Ever.

Besides, she wasn't merely a woman. Valora Belia Merin was a soldier. A warrior. She was tall and strong, trained from the age of five to wield a sword and a spear as well as any soldier. Better than most, her father said. She also handled a bow and arrow with uncanny expertise. When she fought, her eyes took on the many hues of a vivid rainbow, or so she had been told. It wasn't as if she could watch herself fight in a mirror. She was cursed with her father's curly dark hair, but her face was shaped much like her mother's, and when she was not fighting her eyes were Bela green.

According to the mystics who'd foretold of her coming, she was nearly indestructible. That *nearly* had given her mother, Bela Merin, fits for the past thirteen years. She mentioned the annoying word often.

One born, one hatched, one created. Val Merin was the one born. Her father was curious about who the others were and where they might be, but Val was not. She might never know them, might never see them. Her part of the war might be fought in a different part of the country than the others so vaguely named in the prophecy. The "one hatched" was curious, she would admit, and the "one created" was too vague. Everything and everyone were created, in one way or another. She could not concern herself with either of them.

The prophecy was old, older than she was. It had been delivered by a wizard to Val's parents months before her birth, but she got the feeling that it was even older than that. Much older. Not that it mattered.

She was ready. The war had been going on for years, and still she had simply trained for battle.

When she wasn't engaged in training, she waited impatiently, twiddling her thumbs, helping to care for her brothers and sisters, learning to cook...as if she would ever be called upon to prepare a meal. Food was merely for survival. Give her roasted meat and oatcakes and figs, and she could happily live on them forever. She needed nothing more complicated or time-consuming to assuage her hunger.

Val was ready, but the sword she had been hearing about all her life had not appeared. Her mother insisted that it would not be time for her to fight until Kitty showed up.

Kitty. What a ridiculous name for a sword! Of course, to hear Bela Merin tell it, the sword had named herself.

It *was* time. Val knew it to the depths of her soul. If Kitty wouldn't come to her, then she'd have to fetch the sword herself.

Her mother would be so annoyed when she woke in the morning and found that her eldest daughter had left during the night. Her father...she didn't know if her father would be proud or furious. Probably both. They thought she was meant to lead an army, and perhaps that was true. But this first mission, this first fight, was for her alone.

One thing she knew without a doubt. Her father would follow. It was for that reason that Val could not stop. Not to sleep, not to eat. She would only stop to rest her sturdy and steadfast mare. Snowflake should not suffer for Val's decisions.

It was possible that if her father caught up with her, he would offer to assist. It was also possible that he would order her home.

A destined warrior should not have to follow the commands of an overprotective father.

Val looked toward Forbidden Mountain from her place on the road. It was the easternmost mountain in a vast range that seemed to go on forever. Well to the west the Mountains of the North, where Anwyn and Caradon made their homes, rose much higher than the mountain ahead of her.

She was well-armed and had packed enough provisions for several days, and so far her journey was off to a good start. The bright moon lit her way. She'd enjoy riding while she could, as she'd have to leave Snowflake behind before starting her trek up the mountainside. Not even a horse as surefooted as the beloved mare could handle those twists and turns. Val had many cousins in the Turi village at the foot of the mountain. One or more of them would care for her horse while she collected Kitty. They would keep her secret.

They would keep her secret because she was older than they were. She was a leader; they looked up to her. Truth be told, they were also a little scared of her. It was the legend, her demeanor, the wild hair she could not tame, the way her eyes flickered…and an impressive stare she had worked to hone. A death stare, her youngest brother called it.

A stare could not possibly be of any help in the situations that awaited her.

Somewhere in those mountains there waited a daughter of the Isen Demon named Uryen. As a child, Uryen had plotted to stop Val's conception. That was a story she had heard too many times, and ewww, she did not want to think about her own conception. Not that she was ignorant of how it had taken place. She had two brothers and two sisters, so she also knew that her parents had not been chaste since her birth. That didn't mean she wanted to imagine the two of them…again, ewww.

Best to think of Uryen, a child of the Isen Demon, who wanted her dead. A supposedly powerful child of the demon who stood between Val and Kitty. Uryen would be a fully grown woman now. Did she still wait there in the mountains? Was a girl not yet old enough to marry still the focus of a demon's anger?

Val shook off the unexpected tickle of fear that ran along her spine. "I am not afraid," she whispered to the moon above. She squared her shoulders and kept her eyes on the mountain top that was her destination. She would not be afraid of what waited there.

She was powerful, too.

CHAPTER TWO

Traveling into the foothills of the Mountains of the North gave Linara a new appreciation for being alone. Truly, wonderfully alone, lost in the thick brush, under the leaves of towering trees. For the past four years, she'd lived with or nearby Stasio and his believers. Every building of every town housed men and women, soldiers and demon daughters; people on top of people. Sometimes literally. Their numbers had grown steadily as they'd moved from place to place. Linara's only time to herself had been too-short, stolen moments when she'd stepped outside, hiding in the night shadows. In the past year, those moments had been spent waiting for the dragon to appear. Before leaving home, Sophie and Kane and at least a handful of their other children and grandchildren had been close by. Even then Linara's moments of solitude had been rare and cherished.

Now here she was entirely on her own, as she had been for the past three days. There was not a soul for many miles; she knew it to the pit of her soul. Not a demon or a shapeshifter. Certainly not a human, though humans had walked this trail in the past, as she walked it now. On occasion she reached out tendrils of energy, searching for the essence, the *electricity* of life. There was none here, none but her own.

Columbyana and the lands beyond were in a state of chaos. As a daughter of the Isen Demon, and the first and — they said — most powerful of those children, she should delight in chaos. In truth, she delighted in nothing. She found no joy in war.

Until she could manage to leave the teachings and influence of her childhood behind, she could not become who she needed to be. Killer. Demon. Leader of a dark army.

In the days since she'd begun her trek, she'd not yet sensed a gnawing hunger, the need to take the life of a human to sustain her own. That hunger would come, though, and when it did she would track down what she needed. Her first feeding would come from a shapeshifting Anwyn or Caradon, she supposed, since she was in their territory. She was glad of that, that her first kill would come from someone able to fight. It should not be easy to take a life.

She'd walked day and night, with only short stops for rest. Sleep was nice, and she claimed it on occasion, but it was not a necessity. Like so many ordinary things in life, dreams were a luxury. She carried in her sack three small knives, a thin blanket, and a bit of food that would not ease her demon hunger when it came. She would chew upon that food, in any case, out of habit. A wineskin filled with water and yet another knife hung from her belt.

Her traveling outfit was made for comfort and durability. The blue gown was long and loose, belted loosely at the waist, and it had two large pockets. Pockets were so wonderfully handy; it annoyed her that more frocks weren't made with two, or three, or even four. She wore sturdy boots which had, so far, served her well.

Linara had not yet seen or heard or sensed a shapeshifter of any kind. The Anwyn and Caradon only shifted during the full moon, but she didn't fool herself into thinking they might be any less dangerous in human form. She'd make a tempting target for any human or shifter intent on assault or robbery. A small and seemingly helpless woman traveling alone, carrying a pack that might contain valuables, would appear to be an easy mark.

Would it be easier to take the life of one who meant her harm? She would think so. Time would tell, she supposed.

As dawn approached and Linara left the thickest part of the forest and stepped onto a path of stone, she finally sensed a presence she could not identify. It was strong, powerful, like nothing she had ever experienced. And then, as it grew closer, she knew who — what — shared the mountain with her on this chilly morning. The commanding presence took her breath away.

The dragon dropped from the sky, wings spread

wide, mouth open to reveal many large, sharp teeth and a long red tongue. Its eyes were red and black, fiery in the night. The massive wings, iridescent blue and green, were unexpectedly jewel-like in the starlight. The tail, long and powerful and armed with sharp ridges, whipped behind and around it. The colors of the beast were beautiful, a vibrant blend of blues and greens with touches of orange and black. She had never imagined such colors existed, in nature or in imagination. Such beauty.

As its bird-like talons hit the ground on the ridge before her, the mountain shook. Rocks loosened and fell, skittering down the mountainside. Linara did not spare the falling rocks so much as a glance. She was far too entranced by the creature before her.

If the dragon spit fire in her direction she would be dead in an instant. The trees behind her would burst into flame, and together they would burn. It would be foolish to run, to attempt to hide. The creature was massive, strong, powerful. The fire he emitted was dangerous, she knew. She'd not be able to escape it. Even without fire, one bite, one swipe of sharp talons could separate her head from her body, and she'd be gone.

The dragon moved toward her, shifting its weight, craning its long, lean neck, leaning in and taking a long, deep breath. Of her.

In the past year a small number of demons had left the village and traveled into these mountains, for reasons of their own. They had been bored or afraid, or perhaps both. Stasio had known when they'd left, and he'd realized it when they'd died. He'd been certain the shifters had killed them, but what if it had been him?

Yes, *him*. This close, she soaked in his energy. It was as if he had slipped into the edges of her mind and she had slipped into his. She could not understand his thoughts. It was like trying to comprehend a foreign language, trying to make sense of words she had never heard before.

She had been sent to kill the dragon, and Stasio had assured her that it was possible, that she was destined to do so. Looking at him now, hypnotized by his beauty and strength — and oh, those fine colors — she wondered how such a creature might die.

Magnificent, rare — perhaps even the last of his kind — and seemingly impossible to kill.

Stasio pushed into her mind, and instantly her tenuous connection with the dragon ended. The creature backed away, snorting steam that swirled around them both. Did he sense the anger, the ill intent, of the party who had joined them? Linara held her breath. Was fire coming?

The dark wizard's words spoke to her in a clear and precise way the dragon's had not. *You will find a way. It is fate. It is your destiny.*

The beast rose into the air, strangely graceful for one so large and heavy. Fire did come, but it was not directed at her. Instead, a stream of flame shot high into the air, competing with the rising sun. A flap of shimmering wings sent a rush of warm air over Linara, but she did not move. Not even when the dragon turned, and its powerful tail whipped so close to her she might've reached out and touched it, had she been fast enough.

And Stasio's intrusive voice came again. *Find a way.*

Though Val had enjoyed many vacations in the Turi village that was home to her grandparents, uncles, and a large number of cousins, Forbidden Mountain had always been, well, forbidden to her. Duh. Not that she'd ever desired to explore the barren and rocky landscape. It really wasn't much to look at.

But since she'd learned that Kitty had been hidden here before her birth, she'd been dreaming of this moment.

Snowflake was left behind with a cousin sworn to secrecy. With her backpack filled with enough food for several days, a thin blanket, and three knives of varying length as well as one snuggly secured in a leather sheath at her waist, Val was as prepared as she could be. According to Granny, Bela Merin's mother, the magical sword Kitty was lost in a cave that had been blocked by a landslide. Forever lost, no matter what prophecies might say. It was a warning to her granddaughter to stay away, to give up on what she'd been promised.

Val felt confident that she could lead an army with any sword available to her, but the idea of Kitty, the promise of her own magical sword...she had to retrieve it. She had to try.

In her mind, she could see herself leading an army with Kitty in her hand. Ariana Chamblyn had commanded an army, so it wasn't like it was unthinkable for a woman to lead the fight. Ariana was a legend; she was revered. Val didn't want to be a legend; she wanted to do the job for which she'd been destined.

Not that she would mind being a legend one day. If she earned it, of course. If it was meant to be. She was more than a thirteen-year-old girl. She was a warrior, born and bred.

One born...

She was so distracted that she almost missed the scuffle of loose rocks behind her. No one else should be on this trail! The Turis didn't come here. They took the "forbidden" part of this mountain's name seriously. Most of the time. No one lived here. There weren't even animals on this cursed rock! Her mind immediately went to Uryen. Surely that demon daughter hadn't been living on this mountain all these years, waiting for Val to show herself! It didn't make sense.

Still, Val was nothing if not cautious. She placed herself behind a boulder where she was hidden but could peek around and have a good view of the trail. She would see whoever was following long before they saw her. Knife in hand, pack on the ground behind her, Val was ready to fight if need be.

She immediately recognized the pale head of hair as it came into view. She sighed and sheathed her knife.

"Cyrus Bannan!" she said sharply, in her best warrior-like voice.

His head snapped up, and the look in his pale blue eyes screamed *Caught!*

"What are you doing here?" she snapped. He should be working on his father's farm, all muscles and sweat, with that long pale hair pulled back to keep the golden strands out of his pretty face. His hair was soft and straight and silky, everything her own hair was not. His eyes were a fantastic blue, like the sky on a clear autumn day.

Cyrus Bannan was fifteen years old, almost sixteen. He was friends with her cousins, even though he was older than they were by a couple or three years. She had admired him from afar since she'd visited her relatives the summer she'd turned eleven. As far as she could tell, he didn't even know she was alive.

He carried a pack similar to hers, and he also had a knife at his waist. When he looked at her — oh, those eyes...

"Laco told me where you were heading. I didn't like the idea of you traveling up here alone."

Laco, her young, loudmouthed cousin, should have kept his mouth shut. So much for trusting family! "I don't need a bodyguard," Val said, staring at Cyrus's nose, which was nicely shaped but not nearly as distracting as his eyes.

"I disagree."

A warrior could not afford to be distracted. Certainly not by a boy.

Val was on the verge of losing her temper. Truth be told, it didn't take much. She came by her temper naturally; neither of her parents was known for their patience. Quite the opposite, in fact.

"You barely know me! Why would you take it upon yourself to...to...to follow me like a wounded calf?"

Instead of being insulted, he smiled. "Everyone knows you, Val. You're supposed to save the world."

She wondered, for a moment, what it would be like to be invisible. To be an ordinary girl who might or might not have a crush on a boy she barely knew, just because he was pretty. "I can manage on my own." With that, she turned, grabbed her pack, and started walking. She had hopes that he'd give up and go home. No such luck.

"I can be your page," he said, a lilt in his voice. "I'll take watch while you sleep."

Like she wanted him to watch her *sleep*! Gah. "There's no one else on this mountain. Why would I need anyone to keep watch?"

"I'm here. You never know who else might have

the same idea."

He had a point. "So you're volunteering to be my lackey." There was a hint of derision in her voice, as she tried to scare or insult him into going away.

"I said page, not lackey." There was a pause, but she didn't turn to look at him. "But I suppose you can call me whatever you'd like."

"Serving boy," she said beneath her breath, but of course he heard her.

"Assistant," he countered.

"Leech," Val said a bit louder.

There was a short pause, a grunt as he worked his way up and over a steep bit in the path, and then he said, the tone of his voice different than it had been before, "Friend."

She could not respond to that with derision. Val had worked hard all her life to become a warrior. She had trained, and studied, and trained some more. That had not left much — no, not any — time for friends.

This time she did glance back. "You'd better be able to keep up. I won't stop for you."

He nodded, just once, and Val set her sights ahead and up.

Friend. Why did that word make her heart leap?

CHAPTER THREE

She was like the others, the ones that had come before. He'd realized that the moment he'd first laid eyes on her. That look had come from a good distance, of course, long before she'd seen him up close. With his night vision, he had seen her through the tree limbs and leaves as she walked upward and down and up again with purpose. He could've killed her then and there. With a flame born deep in his belly, he could've burned her alive. It would've been easy enough; and not the first time he'd destroyed a daughter of the Isen Demon.

He had not burned her. This newest traveler was very much like the evil women who had come before her, but she was also different. Her essence was not so simple and dark; her thoughts were layered, and went well beyond hate and greed. He needed to know more before he decided if she deserved death or not.

Paxon Raghnall Konrad had always lived on a mountainside. It hadn't always been this particular mountain, but war had drawn him here to this side of the world. War and blood and a search that had taken more than four hundred years of his long life. He had no interest in participating in the wars of men, but war brought energy to the world. Might it also draw others of his kind to this place? If other dragons lived, would they, too, be drawn to the bloodlust of humans?

Was he the last? There were moments when he thought he must be. It had been such a long time since he'd been with others of his kind. In more optimistic moments, he had faith that somewhere in this big world, another dragon flew. Hid. Slept. And perhaps searched for him.

Pax longed for a true mate. A female of his species who would fill the void in his soul, the emptiness he sometimes sensed deep inside on long, cold nights when the world seemed so large, so filled with caverns and shadows that might hide the one he searched for.

He remembered a time when dragons — some like him, some larger, some smaller — had been plenty. They'd lived on the other side of the world on a mountain much like this one. He'd been a small one then, barely able to fly, barely able to belch a spark. He also remembered when the dragon slayers had come, when they had declared war on the beasts they feared. Pax had survived. Perhaps there had been others.

He did not often dwell on that which he most desired, and he did not live his life entirely alone. When he took his human form, he could lie with a woman. For pleasure, for warmth, for companionship. There would be no child of any sexual union with a human or a shifter like those who inhabited these mountains with him, no way to procreate, but he could, for a while, know the comfort and pleasure of sex.

Sex was one of life's most precious pleasures, but he wanted more. He wondered if he would ever find what he searched for.

He had heard of another like him who lived near here, a shifter who took a dragon-like form. She called herself a Firebird, and while she was smaller and weaker than he, they shared many similar traits. She flew; she had fire. While she might look like him, there was one basic difference.

The Firebird's natural form was that of a human. She'd been born to a shifter of these mountains, and she had the ability to transform into a dragon-like creature.

Pax was a dragon who had the ability to shift into human form.

Linara hadn't seen another human for near a week. She liked the solitude, but of course, it could not last. Peace was not for her, not now, not ever.

Though she had headed into the mountains with confidence, the barrenness of the sunlit landscape she now walked upon, the unfamiliar aspect of this land, had begun to worry her. Eventually, she would need to be fed. Unless she could locate and kill the dragon within a few days and turn toward the village where there were people capable of offering what she needed, she would soon know hunger.

She had thought she'd see evidence of the shifters who lived in these mountains here and there, even though she was nowhere near The City or any settlement she was aware of. So far, there was nothing.

As inadequate an archer as she was, perhaps she should've carried a bow and a quiver of arrows with her. The dragon was massive and seemingly hard, but surely he was vulnerable somewhere. The eye. The throat. Beneath his wings. One of her rare and inadequate gifts was a slight increase in speed, but she did not think that would help her in a contest with the dragon.

Stasio had assured her that the beast was vulnerable and that she alone could find his weakness and use it against him. She'd only seen the creature twice since their close encounter on the path three nights ago, and then only from a distance. Did he realize she planned to kill him? Was he afraid?

Of her? No. She doubted such a creature would know any fear.

She felt the energy shift long before she rounded a curve in the rocky trail and saw evidence of occupation. The still warm remnants of a fire; the scent of smoke; tall leather boots sitting by a cave entrance; a sword that was almost as tall as Linara.

A man sat near those boots. He was relaxed, even as he watched her near. He did not seem alarmed, but then why should he? Linara was a small woman. Her demon nature wasn't evident, not at a glance.

The man she approached was larger than most, muscled and — she could tell even though he was sitting — tall. His skin had been darkened by the sun, but that was not surprising, considering how scantily clad he was. He wore no shirt, and the dark gray kilt that covered very little skin was ragged, revealing long and muscular legs. His hair was dark, long, thick, and tangled, and his eyes...those eyes were slanted up at the corners, just a little, and they were as dark as the hair. Darker, perhaps.

At first glance she would mark him as a beggar, he was so unkempt, but there was intelligence in those eyes that captivated her. Intelligence and humor and a challenge she did not understand.

As she walked closer, he stood. Slowly, and with graceful strength. He grabbed a shirt from the ground, a scrap of linen as old and worn as the kilt, and pulled it on. Not that such a shirt served any purpose, other than to conceal an impressive chest. The sleeves had been ripped away or purposely removed. It was difficult to tell what had happened to the poor excuse for a shirt.

The man was even taller than she had imagined, at least six and a half feet tall. His eyes did not leave her as he presented her with a formal bow. His foot jutted out and he dipped, bent appropriately at the waist. One massive, bare arm swept elegantly before him. The attempt was spoiled a bit because his head remained lifted so he could watch her the entire time, instead of turning his gaze to the ground as it should have been with a proper greeting.

"What brings you to my home?" he asked, his voice deep and smooth and hypnotic as he finished with the formal bow and stood tall. "Surely you are lost."

Linara thought a moment before answering. That tremendous sword could easily take her head if she said the wrong thing, and while he was not holding it at the moment, it was nearby. "Yes, I'm lost," she said in a small voice.

The man grinned, revealing strong, white teeth. "And how did that happen, my lady?"

He couldn't just accept her story at face value? No, she was not so lucky. "Do you know of the war with the demons?"

His smile faded. "Of course."

"My family was killed, and I decided to travel to The City of the Anwyn. I have a friend who lives there." An aunt and many cousins, to be specific, but she would not tell him that. No, Juliet and her children and grandchildren were not related by blood. If they thought she was a danger, they would not hesitate to kill her.

"You are on the wrong path, my lady."

Of course she was. The last thing she wanted was to run into a pack of Anwyn! A stray would be convenient when her hunger came, but she wasn't looking for a crowd. "As I said, I got lost."

He studied her, eyes shifting up and down, all pretense of civility abandoned. Just the way he looked at her made her shiver.

"Why would a woman come into these mountains alone?"

"I told you, my family was killed," she snapped.

"You mourn for them?" His gaze bored through her.

"Yes, of course."

He studied her and she knew what he saw. No grief. No remorse. She mourned for no one, and she was not good at pretense.

"If you point me in the right direction, I will disturb you no more," Linara said, eager to be on her way. This man made her spine itch.

A muscled arm lifted, a long finger pointed. The direct route would take her over the side of a sheer cliff.

As the dragon flies...

"You need a guide, my lady," he said as he dropped his arm.

Linara hesitated before answering. A large, strong man would be an asset if she did run into trouble along the way. And if she got so hungry she could not stand it...he would do for her first feeding.

Her heart sank at that thought. She wanted to survive, as any living being would, but she did not want to take a life to save her own. No matter that it was in her nature, no matter that death in exchange for life was a part of her.

The truth was, not feeding wouldn't kill her. At least, not that she'd seen from what had happened to her sisters who hadn't had the protective amulet. She would grow weak, starving for what she needed. She would experience a craving so sharp, so intense, it could not be denied. When the time came, she would feed from whoever was near enough to serve. Even him.

Stasio had not bothered her for days, but he bothered her now, whispering into her head, *Suck him dry if that's what it takes.*

Linara forced Stasio from her mind, rebuilding the shields he'd knocked down.

"I suppose I do need a guide," she said softly. "Are you available for hire?"

Again, that grin. "As it so happens, I am. Do you have gold to pay?"

"My friend in The City, she has gold. I can pay you when we arrive." It was a long way to The City of the Anwyn. It was doubtful her guide would last that long, even if she intended to continue in that direction. She did not want to run into Aunt Juliet and her family! What a disaster that would be.

She walked toward the large man, head high, thoughts protected from the dark wizard who instructed her. "My name is Linara," she said. While she could not manufacture the kind of grin he did, she did manage a small smile. "I would be grateful for your help."

"I will be happy to assist a damsel in distress," he said, and then his eyes caught hers. "My true name is rather long and awkward, but you may call me Pax."

The path up Forbidden Mountain was difficult, but should be no more than a few days' climb. She'd barely started the trek when Cyrus had joined her. For days, she'd allowed him to tag along. He was not a bad traveling companion, Val had to admit. He spoke now and then, but he did not chatter incessantly. He helped set up camp when they stopped for the night. Not that there was much involved in preparing for hours of fitful sleep. Nothing grew here, so there was no shade, no wildlife that might serve as supper, and no fresh water for the past day and a half. There were, in fact, no comforts to be had.

But they each had a blanket to sleep upon, and both carried food and water. A fire would've been nice when the sun went down and the temperature dropped, but there was no wood to gather for such a luxury.

Last night, as she'd drifted toward sleep, Cyrus had spoken to her. She stared up at a sky filled with brilliant stars and a sliver of a moon, her awareness fading, as he spoke of the village where he had been born and had lived all his life. The Turis were a proud and fierce people, born — it was said — of stone, snow, and sunlight. Hard and cold and hot. Val was half Turi, on her mother's side, though her father was quite fierce himself.

She'd never had a chance to be anything other than what she was. Difficult.

Morning had brought a quick return to their hike. There was no need to loiter over their scant breakfast. They walked and walked, forever upwards. At times the path was wide and solid, but there were times when it was necessary to watch each step with great care. Val had given only the briefest glance over the side of the mountain during those times. Cyrus had been silent, too.

The day wore on, slowly and without ease. They should arrive at their destination soon, if her calculations were correct. She should've insisted that Cyrus return home this morning. When she collected Kitty, shouldn't she be alone? Was it right that Cyrus — that *anyone* — be with her?

She shook off the doubts. Every warrior had companions. Squires and other soldiers, perhaps even friends.

Friends. Val had never had one. She loved her siblings and they loved her, but even with them there was a distance that was difficult to explain.

Her life had focused on training in preparation

for this moment. She had no patience for girls who spent their days painting and sewing and giggling like idiots. She despised their pretty dresses and unnecessary jewelry and painstakingly fashioned hairstyles. Heavens save her from poetry! And the boys, well, they were no better. They hated her because she was better with a sword than they were. Better with a sword, and a bow, and a knife. She was faster than they were, stronger, more focused.

Maybe when this war was over, if she survived...

"Do you have many friends?" she asked. Cyrus walked behind her, struggling to keep up, even though his legs were longer than hers and he was accustomed to physical labor.

"Of course. Doesn't everyone?" He sounded naive to her ears.

"Of course," she agreed in a lowered voice.

"All of my friends are from the village," he continued, unprompted. "I haven't been anywhere else, not in my whole life. I know people from school, from seasonal celebrations, and from the market. That's about it, I'm afraid. My life is not nearly as exciting as yours, Valora. You have seen the capital city of Arthes; you have even lived there for a time. Is it a wondrous place?"

Wondrous. Terrifying. Chaotic.

"How do you know where I have lived?" Her voice snapped just a little.

He laughed. "Everyone knows about you. Valora Merin, the promised one. Valora, the child who will save us all." Again he emitted a rough sound that might've been a laugh, but it was deeper than before. Almost serious. "Though I have to say, from my vantage point you look nothing like a child at this moment."

Val's head snapped around and she glared at him. He'd been looking at her ass! How dare he? It was...it was... Her anger faded quickly. It wasn't as though she hadn't admired his form a time or two. She had just not expected anyone to admire hers.

"My family calls me Val. No one calls me Valora." Such a girly name.

"Not even your friends?"

She did not want to admit to him that she didn't have any. "No one."

He nodded, and Val turned her focus to the rocky trail. Almost there. Her parents had told her about this mountain so many times; she felt as if she had already been here. There wasn't far to go before reaching her destination. Her heart sped up, and it had nothing to do with the young man behind her staring at her ass.

The sun had not moved much in the sky before they rounded a large boulder and saw the flat expanse that stretched to a tall, jagged wall of rock.

This was the place. She knew it, not only because her parents had described this part of the mountain many times, but because of the goosebumps on her skin and the increase in her heartbeat. Her mouth went dry. This was it!

Val hurried toward the cave entrance, knelt, and peered inside. The last light of day shone in, and what she saw there, beyond the opening in the rock, caused her heart to sink. Even though she'd been warned, even though she knew what had happened here before her birth, the rubble that blocked her way into the cave where Kitty had been hidden momentarily sucked away all her fine plans.

She reached into the cave, her fingers scraping against cold, hard rock. She could not reach the rocks that had fallen and blocked the entrance, not without crawling inside, but they appeared to be solidly in place.

The sword Val had been promised possessed great magic, or so she had been told. Why had it not cleared the path for her? Kitty was capable of communication, of movement, of power. Did it not possess the ability to move the rocks that separated them?

She.

Val turned her head, wondering why Cyrus had spoken and what that one word might mean. A chill ran down Val's spine. Her traveling companion stood a good distance away, looking away from her, admiring the view from this high vantage point. The word she'd heard had been almost directly in her ear.

Kitty, or her imagination? Magic, or wishful thinking?

She, not it. The voice was there again, and again

it sounded as if someone — something — whispered in her ear.

At that moment, Cyrus turned his head and looked at her. She couldn't wait to tell him...

Tell no one. Trust no one.

"All right," Val whispered. She liked Cyrus well enough, but she did not know him all that well. What if the demon child Uryen had brought him over to her side? With gems or magic or promises of, well, whatever. What if he was a spy for the demon? Best to be safe, she imagined.

She didn't really believe that Cyrus might be anything other than he appeared to be. A farmer's son, on a mission to help a friend's cousin in a time of need. Not that she needed help, but still, his intentions were likely noble. But if she were wrong and he was a spy, could she trust him to accompany her into the cave?

Val squared her shoulders. Kitty was hers. The sword had been forged for her; the grip had been made to fit her hand. No one could take it away. No one, not even a pretty farmer's son with heroic intentions of his own.

"Is everything all right?" he called.

"The way is blocked," Val said. She stood, brushed off her pants, and started walking in his direction. "As I knew, of course." She did not tell him that she'd halfway expected the way to be magically cleared. That would sound like the hope of a child, and she was almost a grown woman.

He smiled at her, and her heart did a little flip in her chest. Why couldn't one of her cousin's uglier friends have come to her aid? No, it had to be this one, with his pretty hair and even prettier eyes.

It was a test. One she intended to pass, as she had passed all tests thrown her way.

So far.

CHAPTER FOUR

Linara soon began to wonder at the wisdom of hiring Pax to lead her higher into the mountains. She'd been told all her life that she possessed a great deal of magic, magic that would come to life as she left the blessing, or curse, of her mother's amulet behind. She'd so far had no problems hiking along these mountain trails, strenuous as the activity might be to many. Weakling? No. Helpless? Absolutely not.

But Pax was taller, stronger, and much faster. His legs were incredibly long. Like it or not, she found herself struggling to keep up.

For the past two nights, she had not seen the dragon. Her plan, such as it was, seemed foolish now. She wasn't strong enough to hurt, much less kill, the beast. Even if she managed to get close, a few flaps of those magnificent wings and the dragon would be so far away she'd never catch up with him.

She had to be honest with herself. She had no plan beyond Stasio's "You will know," which seemed, at the moment, less than a stellar plan. What if she never found a weakness? What if she didn't *know* anything?

She might spend a lifetime here, searching, failing. The beast she sought had no reason to leave these mountains. There were tremendous caves he might hide in, if he wished not to show himself — though she could not imagine he would ever fear her or anyone else enough to hide. Most of the caves they had passed on this trek were not nearly large enough for a creature of his size, but there were some. A few. Enough.

If not for the hunger she knew would come she might not mind a lifetime here, searching for the dragon.

What was she thinking? It wasn't as if there weren't other mountains in the world. If the dragon tired of living here, those wings could take him far away in a very short period of time. In a single night, he could fly to the other side of the world.

This mountain was alternately rocky and barren, and green with life. Their path had taken them through both areas. After a time on unforgiving rocky trails, they had left the more barren segment of the mountain and entered a blessed area where there were occasional trees for shade, water for drinking, and wood for building a fire. Building fires was one of Pax's gifts. On both of the previous nights, Linara had excused herself to empty her bladder and returned moments later to a blazing fire at the center of their campsite. She welcomed the warmth and the light, so she did not question his skill.

After they had eaten a light dinner of dried meat and a tiresome mix of nuts and berries, he settled in a position where the firelight lit his face so well it seemed to glow in the night. Yes, he glowed, and those eyes bored through her, as if he saw all. As if he knew everything about her.

She had brothers — not blood kin, she reminded herself — and she had seen many men in her lifetime. Young and old, small and large, handsome and ugly. But she had never seen one who looked like Pax. His size, the muscles, the fierceness of his features. The slightly slanted eyes. The long, tangled hair that somehow suited him. He was truly a wild man, a creature of these mountains.

Just within the past day, a new hunger had begun to grow within Linara. Though she had never before experienced it, she recognized that hunger for what it was, and wondered if she would end up feeding on this man she admired.

She'd managed to keep the dark wizard out of her head for the entire day, but at that moment, as she regretted what she would eventually be driven to do, he slipped in. Stasio was gleeful as he sensed her new hunger. He reveled in it, as if it were his own. Linara forced him from her head, building a new and stronger shield against him.

She was here to do what had to be done, but she would not allow the wizard to be a part of it. That was the only revenge she could have against him.

If he had not found her, enticed her, drawn her away from home, she would still be the Linara that Sophie Varden had raised to be...what, a good girl? Almost a human woman? It was foolish to imagine that life was possible for her, ever had been or ever would be. The demon would always be within her; it was who she was, who she'd been born to be.

"When are you going to tell me your true purpose here?" Pax asked, that captivating deep voice like silk and gravel combined.

Linara was glad for the interruption. Her thoughts had been leading her round and round. "I told you, I am going to The City..."

"Lie," he whispered.

She drew up, slightly, "How dare you..."

"Lie," he said again, even more softly. "You have a purpose you have not shared with me."

For a moment, she stared at his face. It was a face that intrigued her. Rough, but pleasing. Enjoyable to look upon. Love was not for her, not for any Ksana demon, but she recognized desire as well as she recognized her new hunger.

Linara strongly suspected that Pax would not survive this trip. Strong as he was, he was no match for her. No man, no matter his size, would survive an encounter with her. Her heart sank, her stomach churned. It was already decided, was it not? She would use him, she would feed upon him, and she would walk away.

When that happened, if it happened... when...

she would never be the same. It would be the end of Linara and the birth of the Ksana she was meant to be. She was a poisonous butterfly caught in the midst of an inevitable demonic transformation.

She might as well tell Pax why she'd come. It wasn't as if he'd survive to tell anyone.

"I search for the dragon."

His immediate response was a wide grin. "You do not look like any dragon slayer I have ever seen. You do not even have a sword or a bow."

Linara's chin came up, defiant. Perhaps she did not look strong, but few would be able to match her once she embraced the transformation from woman to demon. It was possible none could. "I did not say I come to slay the dragon."

"What do you want then?" His grin was gone, his dark eyes flashed. "Do you wish to make it your pet? Do you wish to put a collar around the dragon's scrawny neck and lead it into the valley? The beauty and the beast, what a sight that would be."

"Is it wrong to wish to see such a beast up close? Can I not admire a magnificent creature?"

"Magnificent?"

"Yes," she whispered. "I saw him once, and he was indeed magnificent."

"He will burn you to a crisp and crunch upon your bones," Pax promised in a dark voice.

"Why would he? I mean him no harm." Another lie. Would Pax see it, as he had seen her earlier lies?

"It is in his nature to destroy," Pax said. He

leaned forward, moving closer to her and closer to the fire. He had to feel its heat. "We must all be true to our nature, beast or man or woman. Is that not true?"

Her heart sank. "I suppose it is."

"We must each embrace that within us which makes us who we are. Man, woman, or dragon."

Or demon? "Can we not choose to be different?"

"Perhaps for a time, my lady, but nature always wins."

Nature always wins. She wondered if he realized that it was in her nature to kill him with a kiss, to take all that he had in order to feed herself.

Of course, he did not.

He continued, a new, burning look in his eyes. "If you feel the need to tame a wild creature, my lady, look no further than your travel guide. Riding a dragon is risky business, filled with danger and unnecessary risk. Riding me is not nearly so dangerous. I promise, I will not hurt you."

Linara took a moment to be properly shocked, and then she let it go. Here, in this place and in the midst of war, there was no propriety. No rules of courtship, no reason to be coy.

"We will see," she said, and then she moved to her blanket and laid upon it, turning from the man who had propositioned her. An ordinary woman might worry that a man who desired her might try to force himself upon her. She might face her companion so that she could see him coming, if he were so bold.

It would make killing him so much easier, if he were that kind of man. He was not, she knew.

He had promised not to hurt her. That was, in a strange way, almost gallant. She, of course, could make no similar promise. If she agreed to lie with him, he would be near a painful death.

Pax watched the woman sleep. He had never needed much sleep, and from what he had seen neither did she. A few short hours during the night was all she took.

Who was she? What did she want? What did she want with him?

In the past three years, he had defended these paths, had guarded these mountains and the people who lived here. The Anwyn and Caradon left him alone. Some of them worshiped him; others were afraid, though he had given them no cause to be.

The only humans he'd killed in his years here were those who had come into these mountains to attack. Pretty, female demons. Could they rightly be called human? Could she?

Linara was a pretty female, and he saw in her the same darkness he'd seen in the others, only…less. She possessed a goodness they had not, but she was like them in a way he saw more clearly when he was a dragon. Was she a demon? Of course, she was. And yet, she had not tried to kiss him, to kill him. Why had she come here? How was he to know?

Pax rose from his seat on the ground and crossed the campsite to stand over her as she slept. She would be easy enough to kill, in his human body or in his true form. Demon or woman, she was fragile. Everything was fragile to a dragon. Everything but the walls of this mountain.

He turned and walked away from her, rounded a corner in the path, and removed the kilt, which was all he wore on this night. With a turn of his hand, he began to change. He grew taller, wider, stronger. Every cell in his body shifted, and it hurt. It always hurt. His feet became talons, so sharp they left furrows in the rock when he shifted one leg. His neck grew long; his arms changed, blue and green and shimmering. His tail scraped the rocky ground.

His stomach and his throat burned.

When his eyes changed, the night was no longer dark. Colors shifted, the world beyond became brighter, and he could see everything, every small detail for miles around.

A single flap of his wings, and he rose into the air. Another, and he soared. In flight, he was efficient, stronger than any living being. The world was his.

He flew over the campsite and looked down. Linara still slept, unaware that the beast she sought was nearby. She said he was magnificent, that she admired the dragon, but he believed she had a darker motive. What if she did not wish to capture him, but instead wished to end his life? She said she was no dragon slayer, but he didn't believe her. There were more lies in her words than truth.

He needed a closer look at her; he needed to slip into her mind and touch the secrets she fought so hard to keep.

Linara woke when a burst of warm air washed over her. She opened her eyes, the last remnants of a strange dream still with her. Reality returned. The fire had gone out, and there were no stars, no moon. All was black.

Then, the dragon moved. Moonlight danced on those iridescent wings. The moon and the stars had not gone, they had been blocked from view by the massive beast that hovered mere feet away.

She held her breath as the dragon turned his eyes to her. Large, black, and red, angry eyes. If he wished to kill her, he could. He could've killed her while she slept. She never would've known. Death would've simply come and gone while she was caught in a dream.

Perhaps that would be for the best. With a single breath, the dragon Stasio insisted she was meant to kill would end her dilemma.

Fully awake, Linara reached out a hand. As if he knew what she was thinking, what she wanted, the dragon lowered its head. Oh, those teeth were so close. He turned his head to one side, and she placed her hand on his long neck. She caressed gently, though gentleness was not necessary with one as tough as this. The scales were hard, but surprisingly pliable. She liked the feel of him, the shimmer of the moon on his skin. His scent should be unpleasant, as so many animals were, but that was not the case. He smelled of ashes and stone, of water and tall green grass.

She looked to the side, to where Pax should be sleeping. With the fire extinguished, he was lost in darkness. If he woke and looked her way, what would he think to see the dragon hovering above her? What would he think to witness her soft caress?

"Do you know why I have come?" she whispered, wondering if the dragon could understand her, wondering if it mattered. As he had before, the dragon's mind and hers melded momentarily, but she could make no sense of his thoughts. Stasio was not present. Perhaps he slept, or was distracted with other work. Perhaps when the dragon slipped into her mind, there was no space left for the dark wizard.

"I am meant to kill you," she confessed. Why not speak the truth, here and now? "I do not want to." She allowed her hand to drop. "It would be better if you killed me, dragon. I do not like who I am, not anymore. I don't want to do…any of the things I am meant to do in the days to come. Take the choice from me. Burn me."

She should turn away. Perhaps she should cry, a little, for the life she was ready to give up. But she did neither. She looked into the dragon's eyes, waiting for him to end her.

The hovering dragon shifted farther away, wings moving slowly but with grace and power, sharp talons moving dangerously close.

"It must be the fire," she whispered. The talons would hurt, they would rip her to shreds. But unless he took her head she'd survive. She would heal.

The dragon rose up quickly and silently, only offering fire when he was too far away for her to feel the heat. The flame lit the night, streaking across the sky, and then, with a flap of those massive wings, the dragon was gone.

Only then did Linara look again to the other side of the campsite where Pax was sleeping. She half expected to see him standing there, ready to fight, that huge sword grasped in one meaty hand.

But she saw nothing. All was dark and silent. In the shadows of this night, he slept on. In spite of the pounding of her heart, she soon did the same.

She dreamed of dragons.

CHAPTER FIVE

Val had been disappointed to find the entrance to the cave where Kitty waited blocked, but she was not deterred. There was another way in; she knew it. She could hardly get into the cave the same way her parents had exited — via waterfall — but *somewhere* on this mountain was a path to the sword which was destined to be hers.

For days, she and Cyrus had searched. He had come in handy a time or two, she would admit, and he seemed not only willing, but eager to help. It was fortunate that the backside of this mountain was not as bare as the side that faced the Turi village. Here there was vegetation, water, wood for a nightly fire, and plenty of nuts and berries. A person could live here for a long while, if they were so inclined. She was a little surprised that they'd seen no evidence of humans who had come before, though there was the occasional small animal. One night Cyrus had devised a clever trap and caught a *tilsi*, which he had roasted for their supper. Meat! Val had rejoiced in it.

As she'd eaten the roasted, slightly burned *tilsi*, she'd had the thought that perhaps it was a good thing that Cyrus had come along, that she'd not sent him home, as she'd thought of doing more than once. He did provide conversation now and then, as well as food, though he didn't ramble on and on. She'd noted that about him before. It was an asset, in her opinion.

Now and then, Kitty whispered to her. Day or night, alone or in the middle of a conversation with her traveling companion, it didn't seem to matter. The first two or three times the whispering had been startling and, well, weird. As Kitty had insisted, Val didn't tell Cyrus that the sword sometimes spoke words only she could hear.

He already thought she was strange enough. No need to add to that admittedly logical conclusion.

Not long before the sun set, Cyrus built a small fire at the center of their campsite. There was no *tilsi* to roast tonight. They'd have to be satisfied with more nuts and the last of Cyrus' oatcakes for their evening meal. Still, a fire was nice for warmth and light. It had been a long and tiring day, but she needed time to relax before trying to sleep. Her mind was spinning; she knew great frustration. How was she supposed to go to sleep simply because it was dark?

Val herself was perfectly capable of building a fire, but it was nice to have someone along to do it for her. She was tired. All day she'd climbed, searching for a crack in the rock, praying to find a way into the cavern, into the heart of the mountain.

Her legs, which were normally quite strong, ached a bit tonight. Not that she'd admit so aloud.

Kitty was in there. So close, and yet elusive. Why didn't the sword whisper something useful, like directions to the chamber where she waited to be claimed?

No. There was plenty of encouragement, and warnings about not trusting anyone, but nothing so specific as "go to the north side of the mountain and climb up ten feet to the hidden entrance." Wouldn't that be handy?

Val wasn't sure the sword could read her thoughts — it would be creepy if it could — so she whispered in a low voice. "How about some help here?"

Kitty didn't respond, but Cyrus did. He looked up, his annoyingly pretty face well illuminated by the small fire he'd built. "Did you say something?"

Val sighed. Sound did travel out here. "Just talking to myself."

"Oh." Cyrus stood, walked away from the fire, and sat just a few feet away. Why did he need to be closer? She could hear him very well from over there, by the fire. "I've been thinking…"

Uh-oh…

"Maybe you're not supposed to find the sword."

Val sat up tall. She wondered if Cyrus got the full effect of her stare in the near-dark. "I am destined to wield that sword!"

He shrugged. "Yes, but maybe you're too young.

You're only thirteen."

"Thirteen and a half."

"In a few years..."

A few *years*? "No," she snapped.

They were far away from everyone and everything, and for a moment Val was sharply aware of that fact. There was no war here, no danger. The Turis had not been bothered much by the war — they were too isolated — and this mountain was even more isolated than the village below. For a moment, just a moment, she considered... She shook off the unexpected illusion. No! She would not hide away, not for a day longer than was necessary.

"Fighting wars is not for girls," Cyrus insisted. "War is for men, and maybe some grown women, but..."

"You said yourself that I am meant to be a warrior, that I will save people." She could not allow even Cyrus to see her short-lived doubts.

He gave a disgusted grunt. "Yes, but maybe not right now."

Val opened her mouth to tell Cyrus that now was the time, that Kitty had been speaking to her, urging her on. But the warning to keep that to herself nagged at her. "I can't give up," she said in a calmer voice. "This is my destiny."

"It's not fair," Cyrus said, sounding dejected. "When I first joined you I thought I was doing my duty, that I could be a part of something important.

I didn't like you so much then." His chin came up. "Now I do, and I won't apologize for worrying about you."

He *liked* her?

"You should not be a soldier, Valora," he insisted. "You should let a man court you. Marry. Have babies and make a home and be safe. Always. Let someone else find Kitty, if the sword is indeed meant to be found." He huffed a bit. "Maybe the wizards are wrong about you."

He liked her, *and* he thought she should get married and have babies? She didn't know whether to be flattered or horrified. She settled for both.

"I can't quit," she said in a low voice.

Cyrus nodded his fine head. If she ever did get married...no, her mind could not go there!

"I thought you'd say that, but I had to try." He stood, and returned to the other side of the camp where he settled on his blanket. They needed rest; tomorrow was going to be another long, tiring day.

It took Val too long to fall asleep. Cyrus' words stayed with her. A normal life, the life he talked about, was not for her. She had been told that she'd be hard to kill, but in no part of the prophecy did it say she would survive this war. Kitty or no Kitty.

Far to the west, a new light lit the sky. Val sat up slowly, hoping for a better look. She squinted, wondering if the light that had caught her eye would come again. After a few moments, it did. There it was, a brilliant spark in the star-filled sky.

Against all logic, she knew that spark was fire.

And Kitty whispered, *one hatched.*

The days and nights were long ones, as they traversed this mountain. Up one trail and down another. Into wooded areas on occasion, leaving any semblance of a trail behind to make their own way. From all Linara could tell, The City of the Anwyn was well to the north. Pax led her unerringly east and a bit south.

They'd left the blessed, shady woods behind, again, and were on a narrow, rocky path that was treacherously steep in some spots, wider and safer in others. Linara waited until they were on a relatively flat part of the path before she rushed closer to her guide. Heavens, she was tired of looking at that tangle of dark hair and the insufficient linen shirt.

"Where are you taking me?" she asked, struggling to keep pace with him.

"You want to see the dragon, yes?" He did not slow, did not bother to turn to face her.

"Yes."

"I am taking you to his lair." His words were so calmly delivered, so matter-of-fact.

Linara's heart raced. "You know where his lair is?"

"Of course. I have lived in the mountains for many years."

"How many?"

Pax finally stopped and turned to look at her. There was humor in his eyes, strength in his fine body. A part of her wanted to put her fingers in that mane of hair and...but no. That would be the end of him, wouldn't it?

Her hunger grew every day. If he got too close, if he touched her, she would lay her mouth on him and drain him dry.

Not until he takes you to the dragon's lair.

Stasio! She hated that he could sneak into her mind at will, that she could not keep him out without holding a constant shield. She erected that shield now.

"How many years?" she asked again, taking quick steps to catch up to Pax.

"I have been living on this particular mountain a mere three years, but one mountain is much like any other, and it is the terrain I prefer."

She could not see why any man would choose such isolation. Was he hiding from something or someone? Did he simply dislike people? It was curious. She should not be curious... "Fine. How long have you been a mountain dweller?"

"For more years than I can count," he said, before turning to continue along the path. If this rough trail could be called a path at all.

"You are not so old," she said.

"I'm older than I look."

Linara had to work to keep pace with Pax, since

his legs were so much longer than hers, but she did not want to fall behind. Not now, when the conversation had grown so interesting. She should ask about the dragon, but she did not. That would come soon enough.

"Why does a man who is neither Anwyn nor Caradon live in these mountains? I thought the shifters didn't tolerate outsiders."

"They tolerate me."

"Yes, but why?"

Pax didn't answer, and she did not press again. They came to a steep section of the trail, and soon she did not have the air to speak. Her guide must've heard her puffing, or slipping, or cursing beneath her breath, because without warning he turned, walked to her, and lifted her with ease. He proceeded to carry her as if she were a small child, caught in his arms.

"Put me down," she insisted.

He did not. Pax turned and carried her along a steep upturn in the path. "You are tired; I am not. I will carry you."

How did he manage to continue walking so easily with her in his arms? His bag and hers were tied to his back. His sword hung at one hip.

"Guide and pack mule," she said with intentional derision, hoping he would be insulted and drop her. It wouldn't hurt to hit the ground from this distance. Much.

Pax laughed at her and continued on. His eyes

were on the path ahead. Her eyes were on him.

He was too close, the feel of him was too tempting. She responded to Pax in the way any woman might to a man of his magnificence. Her mouth went dry, her insides quaked and fluttered. It was not a surprise, really, that the scent of him, the feel of his arms around her, the nearness of his sun-warmed skin, made her think of what it might be like to…

No. No, no, no. Linara closed her eyes. She could not allow this weakness. Was her sharp desire a part of the demon or the woman? How was she to know?

She wanted him, of course she did, but that wasn't all she experienced. With every step he took, her hunger grew at an alarming rate of speed. It was a hunger she knew without doubt came from the demon.

"I do not need to be carried!" she insisted, balling her fists and pummeling his hard chest. "Put me down this instant!"

He merely chuckled and continued on.

The man who carried her smelled too good; her hunger grew sharper. Her hands gripped his muscular arms. His skin was *right there*. His fine lips were so close. So tempting.

A man like this one would feed her well…and then what? She didn't know where the dragon's lair was, didn't really know exactly where on this mountain she was at the moment. She'd be well fed and hopelessly lost, if she placed her mouth on his now and took all that she needed.

No, not all. Never all. She would always want and need more.

Even though he carried her pack, as he had for days, she had one of her smaller knives tucked at her waist. She pulled that knife and lifted it smoothly. Without hesitation, she placed the sharp edge at Pax's throat. She saw his heartbeat in a vein there. It would not take much pressure to draw blood.

"Put me down," she said again, more calmly this time.

He did, in a move so smooth and quick she lost her breath. She lost her knife, as well. It flew through the air, momentarily. Pax caught it, far too easily. Linara's feet hit the ground, but the slope was too steep, and she ended up on her ass.

He towered over her. From her position — sitting with her legs clumsily spread, unarmed, and breathless — she could see up his scanty kilt.

Apparently, he was amused. Amused and aroused.

It was death to be aroused around a Ksana demon. Pax had no way to know her true nature, of course. He saw a helpless woman, a weak female who was now and always at his mercy.

She moved her gaze upward toward his throat, wondering if in that maneuver he had managed to cut his throat with her knife. There was not so much as a pink mark there, much less blood.

"You are down, as you insisted," he said, and then he offered his hand. "May I assist you to your feet so you can once again struggle to keep pace with me?"

She would argue, but he was right. He had no way to know that she had attacked him for his own good.

At this moment, with her emotions and her needs in turmoil, it would not even be wise for her to take his hand. That hand would be warm and strong. His touch would be...

No, she could not let her mind go there. Linara rolled over, scrabbling in the dirt to come up on her hands and knees. She stopped to take a breath. Pax did not offer again to help her. His massive arms crossed over his chest, and he continued to smile as she struggled to her feet. Once there, she brushed the dirt from her skirt and combed her hair with her fingers. Then she offered her hand, palm up, for her knife.

A sane man would refuse. She had threatened Pax with that knife, she'd held it against his throat. Why would he return it to her?

But he did, slapping the grip into her palm and then turning from her to begin climbing again.

Linara placed the knife in its sheath and followed.

Was the man insane or brave?

***

She was not like the others. Not like other demons, not like other women he had known. Pax turned and looked at the woman who followed him. Who was she? *What* was she? She never complained of the cold, the hardship of the climb, or hunger. Linara was a woman on a mission.

As the others had been.

To most, the daughters of the demon looked like any other human woman. Beautiful, fragile, even helpless. But Pax was not a man; his senses were beyond keen. There was a particular odor about them that set the demons apart. Not an unpleasant smell nor a pleasant one, just different. And when he was in his dragon form, he could see energy around them. Energy that came in waves, and in colors specific to a person's soul. All his life, he had seen this energy, light and dark, and in all colors of the rainbow. He sometimes saw a human's aura when he was not a dragon, but it was an ability that came and went.

As a dragon, the colors that allowed him to see a person's essence flowed without effort.

He had never before seen black in that energy, not until he had flown over a pair of demons killing a couple of Anwyn wanderers. The females had laid their mouths on those of the shifters and had been in the process of draining them. Their energy turned a darker black than he'd known possible as they fed.

His appearance had stopped their killing kisses. One of them had foolishly drawn a short sword, as if that puny weapon could do him harm. The Anwyn beasts had wisely fled as soon as they were free, weakened but able to stumble away.

And when they had been far enough away to be safe, Pax had spit flame at the demons and ended their vicious lives. Then he had eaten them because he was, after all, a dragon. He often existed on wild beasts alone, averse to taking human lives. But these women — and those like them who had followed — were not exactly human. They were not *entirely* human.

Their kisses meant death to men, but he'd had no problem devouring their charred remains. He was tougher than any man. It was not so easy to kill a dragon.

He had intended to eat Linara the first night he had seen her, but her energy was not like that of the others. There was some black, and that was unusual enough for him to know that she was, in many ways, like them, but there were also human colors in abundance. All the colors of the rainbow danced within her. Colors he had never seen before, and in his five hundred plus years he had seen every color imaginable. Or so he had thought.

She had come here to kill him, or so she had whispered to the dragon. She'd all but asked for his fire. Her words had been more confession than statement of fact. So why had he allowed her to live?

He spared her, for now. If she tried to kiss him, though…

"I do not know what a woman might want with a dragon," he said without turning to look at her. He had memorized every line of her beautiful face, every curve of her shapely body, the way the sun and the moon shone on her silver hair. "He cannot be tamed, and he might decide to devour you."

"You are a guide, not an advisor," she answered, her low voice haughty. Did she think she could intimidate him into silence?

"Yes, a hired guide you promised to pay when we reached your friends in The City. Yet we are no longer going to The City, so I am not certain how you plan to pay me. If you have no coin, I suppose we can barter."

She sighed. He smiled.

"How much further to the dragon's lair?" she asked.

"Two days' travel. No more."

Her response was a whispered and tired sounding, "Thank the heavens."

Pax's smile died. What kind of demon spoke of heaven?

CHAPTER SIX

Val's hurry to find a way into the caves wasn't spurred only by her need to retrieve Kitty and get to her destined role as warrior. She knew well her father would come after her, and soon. She was a bit surprised he hadn't found her yet. General Merin — though he had not been an actual general for many years everyone still called him that — was unrelenting in all things. Most especially his love and protection for his family.

After the night when he'd tried to dissuade Val from her mission, Cyrus had become oddly unhelpful. For someone who'd worked his father's farm all his life, he wasn't particularly strong, and since she'd rejected his advice it had gotten worse. Perhaps this adventure had proven to be more difficult, or more lengthy, than he'd imagined. Whenever Val climbed up the side of the mountain which was blessedly green on this side, Cyrus would stay behind, calling out encouragement, but not scaling the mountain himself.

She had never thought him a weakling before, but he had begun to act like one. And to think she had once found him so handsome. He was handsome, still, but he wasn't very manly. Yes, this adventure was wearing on him. Maybe he wasn't meant for anything other than farming and the ordinary life offered in a small village. Was that fair? Did it matter? Life was rarely fair, so why should she be? She did feel some disappointment that he wasn't all that she'd initially thought him to be. Perhaps that's why her observations had turned harsh.

He did climb, though, when Val finally discovered what had to be a narrow entrance to the cave. She knew this was the place because when she put her head into the crevice she heard rushing water. Not far beyond this crack in the side of the mountain flowed the underground stream of rainbows and whispers. She had heard much about that river.

Kitty was in there somewhere. At this moment the magical sword was oddly silent.

Val looked over her shoulder, to watch a huffing and puffing Cyrus move close enough to see the entrance for himself. There was only a narrow ledge for them to stand upon, and soon he stood very near. He was tall, taller than she had noted before now. Then again, they were usually not standing so close. It was disconcerting.

Once they slipped into the crevice it would be dark for a while. How long, she did not know. When they reached the caverns — if this passage did not narrow so they had to turn back — there would be a glimmering light from the stone walls, and from the river, but as they made their way toward her destiny, it would be dark.

Darkness didn't bother her. Would it bother Cyrus?

"You can wait here, if you'd like," she said. "It will be a tight fit, from what I can see."

Cyrus shook his head. "I cannot let you go in there alone. It might be dangerous. You might need me."

Even though he was kind of, well, spineless, and not quite as dashing as she had initially thought him to be, it was chivalrous of him to think of her safety. Perhaps she'd judged him too harshly, and too quickly. "I'll be fine."

He nodded his head once, rather sternly. "I'm coming with you, Val, and that's that."

Maybe he wasn't entirely spineless...

"Let's go."

She led the way, slipping into the crevice and snaking slowly toward the sound of the water. On her belly, using her knees and elbows, she inched forward. It was indeed dark, for a while, but soon she found herself moving toward a strange and beautiful light. There was a faint glimmer at first, just barely touched with color, but with every forward movement that light grew stronger. All was well, so far. As long as the passageway remained wide enough. As long as the opening at the end of this crawl wasn't a hole in a wall too far off the ground to do her any good or too small for her to fit through. She and Cyrus could back out, if they had to, but it would be such a disappointment.

Val scraped her hands, as she pulled herself along. Her trousers caught on a sharp rock and they tore, just a little. Another sharp rock dragged along the newly exposed skin there on her thigh, stinging, drawing blood.

A few scratches and scrapes meant nothing. She'd always been a fast healer. This narrow passage wasn't the worst of the dangers she'd face in the weeks and months to come. It was an insignificant obstacle, no more.

The light grew stronger, brighter. There was a decidedly odd quality to it, which was not a surprise. What drew her forward was a wavering bluish light. Then a purple. Then pink. Nothing about the light from the caverns was natural; she knew that.

Finally, she reached the opening and slipped her head free of the passage. For a moment she was speechless. She even held her breath. In all her life, she had never seen such beauty. The stone walls gleamed with light and life. Rock, smooth mixed with rough, was alive with light that ebbed and flowed, and seemed to have a heartbeat, of sorts. The stream winding through the cavern rushed along, a colorful ribbon leading, she knew, to a waterfall.

A waterfall which might be their only way out. The stream and the waterfall were a part of the story she'd heard all her life. If no other method of exiting this place presented itself, she'd make the jump. Her parents had survived the fall, and so would she.

"Move!" Cyrus said. He sounded annoyed, and she couldn't blame him, not really. His view was of her rear end and her boots, which was not nearly as interesting as *this*.

While the hole in the cavern wall was not so high that it made egress impossible, neither was it going to be easy. Val carefully and slowly eased out and onto a narrow ledge. The ledge was not quite wide enough to accommodate her entire booted foot, but it was sufficient. Barely. There was no evident place to grip the stone, to secure herself before proceeding downward. The fall to the cavern floor might not kill her, but it wouldn't be pleasant, either. The last thing she needed was a broken leg.

She studied the wall around and beneath her and found some small, shallow crevices that might serve as footholds and handholds. Holding her breath, planning each move carefully, she swung herself around and over. The tip of one boot found a cleft. The fingers of one hand gripped another.

Cyrus had worked his way forward so he could look out onto the caverns. He didn't take any time at all to admire the beauty. He merely glanced about as if this were any old ordinary cave; then he turned a scowl to her. "How am I supposed to get down?"

"Watch me, and follow my moves precisely."

She had a plan, a route in mind. The drop from the final foothold that she could see from her vantage point was no more than eight feet off the ground. With care, and a little luck...

Cyrus did watch her closely. He watched as she slipped and barely caught herself. He watched as she hugged the wall and searched for the next tenuous toehold. Finally, she reached the final crevice. Val took a deep breath and jumped, landing, as always, like a cat. What a relief!

Her companion, her *friend*, did as she'd instructed and made his way down. He was slower than she was, and once she heard him utter an absolutely filthy phrase which shocked her, but finally he reached the last hold and after taking a deep breath, he jumped.

Cyrus did not land as gracefully as she did, but then he had not been trained from birth for this mission.

Again, he muttered a curse she had not expected, but he recovered quickly and stood, giving her a shy smile. "My apologies. I should not say such words in front of a lady."

No one had ever called her a lady! Warrior, destined one, pain in the ass. But never lady. At that moment she forgave him his imperfections.

"Which way?" he asked.

Val looked at the river. It flowed toward the waterfall, which meant that Kitty had been secured in the opposite direction.

She pointed. She and Cyrus both shifted their packs into more comfortable positions and started walking.

Kitty was in here somewhere, but Val had no idea of the precise location.

She took a few steps, then stopped to look up at the crevice in the wall. She wondered if that might be a way out, one safer than the waterfall. It could also serve as a marker, in case they found themselves lost.

The crevice and the holds they had used to climb down were gone. The wall she searched sparkled with color and light, and was as smooth as the cavern floor she stood upon. The opening in the wall, the one she had so recently crawled through, was gone.

She borrowed one of Cyrus' words.

The air was cooler here. Thinner, perhaps. Linara found that she liked it more than she'd expected she would. The coolness. The quiet. She even liked the spots of snow. The snow was melting with the new spring warmth — even here. It remained in shady spots, here so high the cold of winter hung on as long as it possibly could.

She could not deny that the view from the top of the world was exquisite. Pax spoke on occasion, but not without purpose. He went for long stretches of time without uttering a word. So did she. They moved along in an oddly comfortable silence. He did not insist upon carrying her again.

Linara was not alone, she had her guide, but she felt apart from the rest of the world. It was…peaceful.

For the past four years she'd lived in the company of others like her, their servants and their victims, Stasio and others of his kind. She had never been alone, not really. She had never known peace. No wonder she had so enjoyed her nightly excursions to look up at this mountain and the dragon.

For a moment she turned away from Pax and looked outward. The village that had been her home for so long was out of sight, and had been for days. The Southern Province where she had been raised was so far away, it might as well not even exist.

Thinking of the Southern Province naturally made her think of her mother, Sophie. A powerful witch, Sophie and her sisters could have tracked Linara and imprisoned her. For her own good, they would say. To protect her. But they had not.

Not because they didn't care, she knew that. How many times had Sophie told Linara that for good or for ill, she had to choose her own way?

She had chosen her own way, hadn't she? She had chosen her demon sisters, as well as the evil she had learned to accept was in her blood. It had been hard, but she'd willingly thrown off the blanket of false security her family had always provided. Had that been a mistake? How much had Stasio's invasions into her mind influenced her? In truth, she had never entirely accepted either part of herself, not the human or the demon. She'd been caught in between, denying both halves of herself. That denial was a luxury she could not keep for much longer.

She'd been so young when she'd run away from home, so naive. At sixteen, every problem had been momentous. She'd seen no way out, no other viable option. How many times had she looked at her adoptive parents and experienced an intense jealousy? Their love, for one another and for their family — including her — was deep and abiding. And it was something she could never know, no matter which part of herself she chose to embrace. No man could truly love her. She could not lie with a man or give birth to a child. It had seemed she had no choice but to accept her demon nature. Now, four years later...

"I'm sorry," she whispered, her words deeply felt and directed at her mother, her father, the family she had betrayed when she'd run away from home. "I wish I could go back." But she could not undo the impulsive actions of a confused girl who'd been searching for her place in the world.

For a moment, one precious moment, she was almost certain her mother spoke to her in response. Not in actual words Linara could hear, but in waves of emotion. Accepting her apology. Sending love and forgiveness.

Could everything be forgiven?

"We will stay here tonight," Pax said.

Linara tossed off her introspection and turned. Pax stood near a narrow but tall cave entrance, a jagged fissure in the rock. "Can't we continue? We must be close."

"We are very close," he said. "Tell me, Linara, do you have a plan? What will you do when you find yourself face to face with a dragon?"

Stasio had told her, more than once, that when the time came she would know what to do. But she had seen the dragon up close twice now, and could think of no way she might harm it, much less take its life. Quite the opposite, in fact. The dragon was too big and strong for her to take on, and too beautiful to sacrifice.

The dark wizard had not intruded into her mind for more than a day now. Nothing. Not a whisper, not a sigh. It wasn't distance that interfered, she knew. When he'd been in Arthes and she'd been in her bed in the Southern Province, he had spoken to her and had invaded her dreams often. In these mountains, though, his voice had become fainter, and now he was blessedly silent.

She could live here forever, free from him and free from the decision she'd been wrestling with. Who was she, woman or demon? Was she truly destined to embrace her demon blood, or could she deny her birth and choose for herself who and what she would be?

If she had not impulsively tossed away her amulet, she could stay here. She could live high on the mountain with the world spread out before and below her. But she was already hungry, and there was no one around for her to feed from but Pax.

What would happen if the hunger grew and she did not feed? She would not die, she knew that, but she would know nothing but a relentless gnawing not in her stomach but in her soul. Perhaps it would drive her to madness; she did not know. Ksana demons were not known for their self-sacrifice. To her knowledge, none had suffered for more than a day or two of hunger without taking what they needed.

Her need had not reached an unmanageable stage, but it would. The time would come when she would not be able to stop herself from laying her mouth on Pax's and drawing out every last drop of his life force.

"You can leave me here," she said, attempting to make her voice cold, distant. She was good at putting on the ice queen front, in facial expression and in voice, even as her heart beat too hard and her mind spun in all directions. He had been good to her. He did not deserve to die.

"I have not yet..."

"I'm close enough to the dragon's lair," Linara interrupted. "I will find him." Or he would find her.

Perhaps that would be for the best. The beast had allowed her to survive until now. It was unlikely to happen a third time.

Linara was oddly at peace with the idea of her coming death. She would not take her own life, and when the time came she would likely fight with all she had. It was a natural instinct, survival. And still, battle with a dragon seemed to her to be a fitting way to meet her end.

Pax shrugged wide shoulders. "I will head down the mountain tomorrow, then. Might as well get a good night's rest before turning back." He jerked his head toward the cave. "I come here now and then, and I have left supplies behind. Furs, some dried food. There's a small pond just down that hill, if you wish to bathe or refill your water sack." He pointed. "The water will still be cold, I'm afraid."

She would feel better if he was gone, away from her, away from the danger of her hunger. But there was no logical reason for her to insist that he leave immediately. It would be dark soon. She would sleep, and in the morning he would move on.

"Tomorrow, then," she said, and she walked past him and into the cave, where it was cool and quiet, and the walls sparkled with a quartz she had never seen before.

The deeper she walked into the cave, the more that stone lit the space that should be dark as a night with no moon or stars. Pax was close behind her, and she asked in a lowered, awed voice, "What is the light in the walls?"

"Dragonstone," he said. "Very rare and precious, and only found here and in some areas in the land of the Turis." He pointed in a direction that was likely east. She was too turned about to be certain. "We are not that far from their mountains. Down and up again, and we would be there."

They turned a corner, and Linara found herself in a massive cavern. There were signs of life here. The furs Pax had mentioned. A bowl and a cup. Boots, much like the ones he now wore. A pile of rags that might be another kilt, or two.

There was no sign that a fire had ever been built here. No ash or firewood, no kindling stored against one wall. Perhaps the dragonstone was flammable, or else Pax only came here in the warmer months. In winter, such a place would be beyond cold.

The dragonstone in the walls sparkled. Lights of all colors twinkled and danced and shimmered. All around her, in the walls and the floor and even far above, that light came alive.

"It likes you," Pax said with some amusement.

"How can stone like or not like...anyone or anything?"

He smiled. "Not everything can be explained with ease. You must learn to see beyond what you know to be true."

She didn't argue with him. Not today. Instead she turned around and around. She looked for patterns in the colors, for answers in the stone. And in the end, she simply accepted that while she'd thought nothing could compare with the view of the world from the great height of this mountain, this sight entranced her just as strongly.

Linara had seen much beauty, as well as ugliness, in her lifetime. She'd marveled at sunrises and sunsets, at fields of flowers, at the beast she had come to these mountains to kill. She had never seen anything to compare to this.

Pax leaned forward and whispered, his mouth near her ear.

"Welcome to my home, lady."

CHAPTER SEVEN

Linara was more beautiful than ever, by the light of the dragonstone. It was as if she were caught in a melding of starlight and rainbows. The colors suited her. This mountain suited her.

Pax shook his head. That was a romantic thought, and he was not a romantic being. Linara was a comely woman with an alluring shape and a sharp tongue. She amused and confused him. He wanted her in a way he had never before wanted any woman. All that aside, he could not forget that attractive as she was, she *had* come here to kill him.

And he had brought her to his home. That was not the wisest thing he'd ever done.

Pax had known many women, but he'd never brought one to this place. No, his nights here were spent in solitude, whether he was dragon or man. Perhaps one day he would find a mate and he would bring her here. This would be their home. But a relationship with a human that went beyond a single night? No. He had never before even considered such a thing.

He saw Linara more clearly here, washed in the magical light that was, in many ways, his own. The darkness he had seen in her was real. The black was not as prominent as that in the demons he had killed, but she was one of them. He must not forget that.

She could kill with a kiss.

She could not kill *him*, not in that way. Even in his human form, he was far harder to kill than any ordinary man.

He wanted her. He had wanted her since the moment she'd walked into his camp. Perhaps even earlier, when he had faced her as a dragon and she had been bravely and foolishly unafraid.

"Tell me why you search for the dragon."

Linara had been studying the stone walls of his home but turned to face him as he asked his question. She hesitated before answering.

"Is it not enough to desire to see such a magnificent creature up close?"

"No."

"What if he is the last of his kind, and I will never again have the chance to see…and—"

She stopped speaking abruptly, perhaps because she realized that he could see the lie in her. Her face fell; her eyes widened. Were those tears sparkling in her eyes? Perhaps. Then again, perhaps it was a trick of the dragonstone.

"You have come to kill him."

"Yes," she whispered, the word echoing off the walls in a way their previous words had not.

"Why?"

Anger flashed in her eyes. The tears, if they had ever existed, were gone. "There is a war in the lands below, are you not aware?"

"I am aware."

"You are capable, why do you not fight? Why do you hide here in these mountains?"

"It is not my war."

"Well, I fight." She slapped a hand against her chest. "I am a soldier, and killing the dragon is my assignment."

"You do not look like any soldier I have ever seen." He took a step closer to her. The cavern was not a small one, but suddenly the space seemed tighter than before, as if the walls were closing in on them. "Women should not fight the wars of men."

"It is not entirely a war of men," she whispered as he stopped directly before her.

Pax took her chin in his hand and made her look him in the eye. What he saw there was a mixture of wonder, horror, and hunger. He lowered his mouth toward hers, intending to kiss her, but she turned her head before their lips met and said, in a tortured whisper, "Don't."

He did not move away. "Why not? Surely a kiss is not too much to ask, as you have no gold with which to pay me for my services."

She turned her head so that their mouths were close, so close. She held her breath for a moment, and then she whispered, "You do not know me. You do not know me at all." Her hands shot up to touch his face, to hold him in place. She was surprisingly strong. "You want to kiss me, but you do not want that kiss more than I do. I crave it. I hurt with wanting it. At this moment, I feel as if I will die without it."

"Then kiss me."

Her eyes met his, and he was surprised to see tears — real tears, not a trick of the light — fill her eyes and then fall down her perfect cheeks. Gods, he could see the pain in her. The wanting and the fear and the sorrow.

"If I kiss you, you will die." She dropped her hands. "Run."

Pax did not run, as he should've. He gathered Linara close and kissed her cheek. He tasted her tears and felt the lurch of a sob she tried to hide from him.

"You cannot kill me with a kiss."

"I can and I will, if you don't…"

He rubbed his beard-roughened face against her soft cheek, then with a hand on her chin he shifted her face so that his mouth was almost on hers. Almost. So close. The air between them shimmered, as if a summer storm lived between them. He whispered, "Prove it."

She fought him at first, but not very hard. Her lips molded to his and he felt her power, lightning coursing through her and into him. Through him and into *her.* He had kissed many women in his very long lifetime, but none had felt like this. He did not back away from the lightning, but embraced it. This was a powerful woman, perhaps the most powerful woman he had ever known.

She was cursed with demon blood; she was a killer of men.

But not, apparently, a killer of dragons.

He speared his tongue into her mouth, and she copied him. He sucked gently, and she moaned.

Her body pressed to his; her fingers slipped into his tangled hair.

At this moment she was only a woman. Warm, welcoming, tempting in a way he had never known before. He could lie with her, here and now. She would not object. She would gladly spread her legs for him; she would take him in.

But did he dare lie with the woman who had come to these mountains to kill him? She had warned the man to run, hoping, perhaps, to spare his life, but once she knew he was not entirely a man...

Linara was the one who ended the kiss, jerking away. She looked at him with wonder and fear, shaking her head and backing away one step. Two. "You should be dead."

He smiled at her. "Your kiss is not so powerful."

"You don't understand..."

"Your father was a demon," he whispered. "I know." He considered being honest with her, here and now. He could say *I am the dragon you seek* and show her his back, the one part of his body that never entirely shifted. He wore the annoying shirt to cover the ridges along his spine from any casual glance, but if she saw, she would know. He could bring a touch of the dragon into his eyes. He could show her his true self, filling this cavern from wall to wall and cooking her where she stood.

He did not.

"How do you know?" she whispered.

"You are not the first of your kind to come to these mountains."

For a moment she was afraid of him. Then the fear passed, and she started asking questions. "What happened to them? Did the shifters kill them? Did you? How do you know so much about the daughters of the Isen Demon?"

"The dragon ate them," he said. "After a thorough cooking, of course. He likes his women crispy," he added in a lowered voice. "As to how I know…just because I live an isolated life doesn't mean I am entirely ignorant of what goes on below. There are travelers to these mountains who escape the dragon's fire, and they are always eager to talk."

"Why aren't you dead? My kiss…"

"Is perhaps not as lethal as you have been led to believe. The others you sucked the life from must've been unusually weak."

Even by the faint light of dragonstone, he saw her pale. "I have never killed a man, with a kiss or in any other way. You were to be my first. I failed."

He moved closer and smiled. "Care to try again?"

She was no longer hungry. Somehow Pax had fed her well, and yet he had survived. He had not only survived; he seemed to be entirely unaffected.

Linara tried to make sense of it all. Perhaps the effects of the amulet lingered, and she was not yet at her full strength. No other powers had manifested. Curious, she tried to start a fire on her palm. Many of the Ksana demons could control fire, to some degree. When that failed, she focused on a pebble several feet away, trying to make it move with her thoughts. That attempt had failed as well. She could not even spark a bit of witch's light on her palm.

Not that she was a witch. Any light she produced would be demon's light.

Perhaps she'd be better off trying to call the darkness upon herself during the day.

Most powerful of her kind? That's what she'd always been told, but it seemed to her that she was the weakest of the Ksana demons.

When she'd run away from home, she had been filled with a young girl's sense of destiny, of purpose. Every hour of every day had shown her all that she could not have. Love. Family. She would never be a part of a loving couple, never be wife to a husband who adored her. So what choice did she have but to become fully demon.

She'd planned to turn on the family who had raised her, and embrace who she was. What she was. As she'd walked away from her home in the dead of night, she had seen herself as a rebel. In the years since, she'd wondered at the wisdom of that decision. Linara Varden was no rebel. In the years since she'd left home, she'd never once thrown off her humanity and become a monster.

Stasio, who had once seemed so dominant and wonderful to her, had proven to be manipulative and power-hungry. He was an almost ordinary man with just enough dark power to make him want more. He might even be called petty. Insignificant. He would kill her if he sensed that thought from her, as he considered himself to be anything but insignificant.

Many of her sisters who followed the dark wizard all but worshiped him. They saw him as a father as well as a leader, and he had fed that image. He liked being worshiped, but he didn't deserve it. He had certainly not deserved her devotion. She could not deny that he had once been more important to her than he was now.

If he sensed her thoughts… With a start she realized that he could not reach her here. Her mind was protected, her thoughts were her own. She opened her mind, reached for him and found nothing. Instinctively she knew it was the stone, the blessed dragonstone, that allowed her to be free from Stasio, and any other who might intrude into her mind. He would have to be content to harass the other Ksanas while she was here. He said they were her sisters, and in many ways that was true.

She should love a sister, the way her mother loved hers. But Linara felt no love.

So many of her *sisters* seemed to have no soul. They were not conflicted, as she was. They were content to kill, to take, to deny the human half of themselves.

She sat against the wall, entranced by the dragonstone's light as she pondered her life. Pax sat beside her, seemingly content to allow her to ponder in blessed silence. He had offered to allow her to kiss him again, as a test. So far, she had refused, but she did want to know if the first kiss had been a fluke.

"If I kiss you again..."

"When," he interrupted. "*When* you kiss me again. Such a kiss should not be a singularity."

"Fine. When I kiss you again, you must promise me that you will move away if you begin to feel ill."

"Your lips upon mine do not make me feel ill. Quite the opposite, Linara. They invigorate me." He turned his head and looked at her, and she was reminded again of his great size, of his strength. If any man could fight against the draw of a Ksana, it would be Pax.

"Promise me," she whispered.

He nodded once.

It might be best to test another kiss now, when she was not hungry. Wouldn't it be easier to move away if she was not drawing in much-needed sustenance? She crawled onto his lap, surprising him. He was a large man, rough-looking, dark, so strong. If anyone could fight against her, it was Pax. She took his face in her hands and gently, cautiously, placed her mouth against his.

He had such fine, full, firm lips...

Instantly she was drawn in, captivated. How could a man be so strong and yet so gentle? How could a man who at first glance appeared to be a brute, kiss with such tenderness? His arms snaked around her; he held her close. He held her tight, but not too tight. There was a sound from deep in his throat. A growl, of sorts. She liked it.

And then the kiss was not so gentle, not so tender. There was demand in the kiss, heat and passion and wanting. He held her tighter; his heat enveloped her.

It was Linara, again, who ended the kiss. The arms that held her relaxed, a little. She did not immediately leave Pax's lap, but looked deeply into his dark eyes. She was searching for evidence that he had been affected by her touch. He had been, but not in the way she had expected.

She scooted off his lap and again sat beside him. Pax leaned toward her and whispered, his voice gruff, "When you are ready, say the word. Call to me, and I am yours. Lie with me, be my woman, and

I will protect you from those who would do you harm, no matter who they might be." He touched her face and made her look at him again. "I am not afraid."

The words caught in Linara's throat so that she could not say aloud those words that came to mind.

I am.

CHAPTER EIGHT

"I'm hungry," Cyrus said, almost whining. Val sighed, leading the way deeper and deeper into the cave where Kitty was hidden. Heaven above, had she ever thought Cyrus manly? Had she ever found him at all appealing? She'd been right to start this quest alone, and that was how she'd have to finish it. Once she had Kitty and they were out of the cave, she'd leave Cyrus behind. Maybe she'd be a coward and slip away in the night, as she had when she'd left home. Then again, maybe she'd order him to go, and he would.

One born, one hatched, one created. Perhaps there was a reason for all those ones. Were they meant to be alone, always? Were they destined to always and forever be *one*?

If she survived the war in which she was supposed to play a part, then she could think about boys and perhaps marry, one day. If she survived, she could put aside her life of purpose and training and singular focus. But only *if.* Not every warrior survived. Far too many of them did not.

"Did you hear me?" Cyrus said. This time, he *did* whine.

"Yes. You are hungry. I am hungry. Our

supplies are meager. We must ration what food we have. Once we're out of here, we'll hunt, and we will eat until we are full."

He sighed. Sighed! Gods, she did not remember him being such a *girl*.

They walked alongside flowing water which sparkled with color and light until that stream took a turn and disappeared into a crevice. The walls still gleamed, but as they moved away from the water, the cavernous space became darker, more shadowed. It was as if they walked in starlight, instead of bright moonlight. There were darker shadows here, and she could not see as far ahead as she'd been able to do before.

Cyrus was probably frightened, but he said nothing. And she did not ask the question, which would surely bring on more complaint.

She should have left him on the side of the mountain, near the short-lived entrance to this magical place. But she had not. Pity.

The water was well behind them when Cyrus gave a startled gasp. Val unsheathed her knife and spun, but she soon returned her weapon to its place. Cyrus was on his knees, reaching into a dark crevice and coming away with a handful of oddly colored mushrooms. And then another. Maybe it was the light, not the mushrooms themselves, but they didn't look like anything she'd consume unless she was truly starving. Nothing edible was that shade of blue! And the green ones looked as if they were slimy. That orange? Gross.

"I haven't had these in years," Cyrus said, plopping down and studying his bounty. After a moment, he dropped both handfuls in his lap.

When he lifted one reddish-orange mushroom to his mouth, Val shouted, "No!" The word seemed to reverberate off the walls, to echo along the entire mountain.

Ignoring her, Cyrus bit off a large chunk of the mushroom, then he lifted the fungus up, offering it to her. "It's delicious," he said.

Val took a step forward. Cyrus did live in this part of the world, and while the mushrooms he had collected looked odd to her, he didn't have a problem eating them. And like him, she was hungry. She just didn't complain about it. She took another step toward Cyrus and the offered mushroom, and then she jerked to a stop. Her hand rested over the knife at her waist.

Sitting in that dark corner, his eyes flashed. Not blue, not the rainbow colors of the stone around them, but red. Demon red. Val blinked, and it happened again.

And Kitty whispered, for her and her alone.

Demon. Run.

There were many things Linara had never expected to know. A true kiss was one of them. Sex? Impossible. Or so she had always believed.

Pax had reclined on one of his furs a while back. Heavens above, he was long and muscled, intimidatingly tall even when lying down. He'd closed his eyes, and his breathing was deep and even, but she did not believe him to be asleep. It was as if she could feel his awareness. As if she were washed in it. They were connected in a strange way.

Did he know what she was thinking?

She scooted closer to him so that she shared the fur he had made his bed and basked in his warmth. This close, she felt so small, so powerless. She might be small, but powerless? Never.

Pax was a large man, perhaps the largest she had ever known. Most of the men in her family were of average size. Pax was not at all average. He was impressive in many ways. There was a wildness about him that appealed to her, as if she were an ordinary woman who might choose a man for herself.

She placed her hand on his bare chest, and his eyes drifted open. He was not alarmed; he had not been sleeping.

"I cannot sleep," she whispered.

"Neither can I." His response was as softly spoken as hers, though there was not another living being for many miles.

"Why can't you sleep?" She held her breath as she awaited an answer.

"I want you beneath me and around me," he answered simply. "That is all I can think about."

"I have never been with a man," she confessed. "I don't know that I can, not without...not without danger to you."

"Because you are Ksana."

"Yes. I am poison."

"Your kiss did not injure me. Perhaps you are not as deadly as you have been led to believe."

If that were true...she held her breath, wondering, waiting, wishing...

Pax wrapped an arm around her, and in one smooth move she was beneath him. His large body crushed hers, but not too much. "And if you are that deadly, well, I can think of no finer way to leave this earth." He smiled, a brilliant, sexy, alluring smile.

She loved that smile. Well, she liked it a lot. She wasn't capable of loving anything or anyone. It was not in her nature. And yet, she did like Pax very well. He was kind and caring. He was strong and handsome. He did not seem to care at all that she was what she was.

He wore nothing but a loose kilt. She'd shed her gown before lying down to sleep, and wore only the thin under-shift which was loose enough to be removed in a flash. If she was going to do this, she wanted nothing between them. Nothing at all.

"If I hurt you, we will stop instantly," she whispered.

"Words I never expected to hear from a beautiful woman," he teased.

Linara could not tease, she could not engage in

lighthearted banter. This moment was too important. She found the fastening at the side of his kilt and fumbled with it. "I want you naked."

His smile faded. "You shall have all that you wish for tonight."

Before she had a chance to turn and run, Val blinked again and Cyrus — not Cyrus — flickered. For a brief moment a woman sat there, and then it was Cyrus, and then, again, it was not.

Val held her knife ready. The woman who was not Cyrus and likely not a woman, either, stood. The mushrooms she had collected fell to the cavern floor, landing silently and rolling away.

"You see me," the stranger said. "The magic of this cavern speaks to you; it allows you to see beyond my magic. I should have known."

"Who are you, and where is Cyrus?" Val snapped.

"I am Uryen. Perhaps you have heard of me."

The demon who'd lived in these mountains since childhood. The demon who had attempted to kill Val's parents simply so Val would never be. "Where is Cyrus?"

The demon did not surge forward, as Val had expected she might. "Find the sword and give it to me, and perhaps I will tell you."

"No."

She does not move toward you because she is

afraid. You are destined to kill her. She fears you.

Val was not comforted by Kitty's whisper. "Cyrus," she said simply, biting out the word.

Uryen shrugged her shoulders. Her eyes glowed red again, and so did her hair. It was as if flame danced there, among the strands. "Dead, maybe. Perhaps stunned by the rock with which I bashed him over the head." She demonstrated, swiping a fist at the air.

"Where and when?" Val asked, while in her mind she tried to remember precisely where on this mountain they'd been when Cyrus had changed. Why hadn't she paid more attention! Why had she moved blindly forward without even noticing?

But she had noticed, hadn't she? She'd been so intent on her goal — Kitty — that she'd dismissed all other concerns.

Uryen took a step closer, and her face fell into the light. She was what anyone would call beautiful. Her skin was pale and flawless. Her hair was an unusual and vivid red, touched with that fire. She had a woman's shapely body, and long, slim fingers. "Give me the sword, and I will tell you. You are supposed to be the end of me, but without the sword you are nothing. I want it for myself. If you gift it to me, if you command the sword to accept me, then perhaps I can allow you to go free."

Val didn't believe that, not for a moment. Uryen was not going to let the warrior destined to take her life survive. The demon must want Kitty badly to allow Val to make it this far.

"Kitty for Cyrus," Uryen said in a sing-song voice. "Give me the sword, and I'll tell you where he is, and then I'll let you go. Promise."

As if a promise from a demon meant anything!

They heard the disturbance in the air at the same time. Both of them reacted, turning toward what sounded like wind and rain and lightning, a storm inside the cavern, moving closer at an alarming speed.

Kitty.

I am yours. You cannot give me away.

As if I would even consider it!

Val held out her free hand, and in an instant, the crystal grip of the sword her mother had claimed many years earlier slapped into her palm.

There was a sense of wonder and relief that washed through Val's body as the sword became a part of her.

Uryen cursed and disappeared. Poof, as if she had never been there.

Val spun around, searching, but she was alone. There were no retreating footsteps, no far-off whispers. She was...no, not alone. She had Kitty.

She lifted the sword so she could see it from end to end. The crystal grip gleamed, and so did the blade. The colors of the cavern were drawn to it, and into it. Such magic. Such wonder.

We have a war to win, Kitty whispered.

"I must find Cyrus first."

He is unimportant, irrelevant.

"But..."

Irrelevant!

"I can't move on until I know," Val said softly. Yes, many lives were at stake, and perhaps one might seem insignificant. But Cyrus was not insignificant to her. He had joined her to help, and she could not abandon him. She could not leave him behind. "He is my friend. Show me the way out of here so we can get started."

She had not known a sword could sigh, but Kitty did.

Linara had never thought to feel a man's bare body against hers, and the sensation was surprisingly delicious. It was more than Pax's warmth, it was the texture of his skin, the way his heart beat, his breath on her neck as he kissed her there.

It was so beautiful, she might think this a dream. But it was no dream, it was reality. A reality that might not last, and yet...

He shifted; his hands gently spread her thighs. He touched her there, where she was already wet for him, where she ached for him. Pleasure so intense she caught her breath whipped through her. She wanted him inside her, but at the same time she didn't want *this* to end. He stroked her as he kissed her throat and then the valley between her breasts.

He slipped a finger inside her while he sucked on one nipple.

If he entered her and found her touch was truly poison, would she be able to stop? Would he? She would gladly risk her own life for this moment. Would she risk his, too?

Yes. Selfishly, she would.

And yet… "If I hurt you," she began.

Pax did not allow her to finish. He growled, shifted, and entered her. His movements were slow but forceful, determined but gentle. And beautiful. Heavens above, so beautiful. To be joined with another, to experience such pleasure, was a joy she had never thought to know.

He was inside her, fully, completely, and she found herself on the edge of something more. Pax moved, and she moved with him, urging him deeper, catching her breath, gasping as he brought her nearer and nearer to something she did not understand. She was driven to get to that place, determined to reach the destination.

And then she did. Intense pleasure ripped through her. She screamed, her body shook and convulsed inside and out, wave upon wave. When he joined her, she felt that, too. He did not scream, as she had, but he growled again.

Pebbles were loosened from the walls around them. They fell with a sound like rushing water in the distance. The light in the cavern changed, brightened then dimmed again.

Linara gasped. She was boneless, worthless, and completely sated. Pax rolled off her, but still cradled her in his arms. Their legs were entwined; their breath came heavy.

She touched his face. "Are you..."

"Alive? Barely." And then he laughed.

"That's nothing to joke about," she said lightly. "You know what I am."

"You are the child of a demon come to kill the dragon. You are poisonous to some, but not to me." He lifted his head and looked at her. "And until we decide otherwise, you are my woman."

Pax watched Linara sleep. He should know better than to lie with a woman who had come to his mountain to end him, but she was tempting. Amazing, really.

All his adult life — hundreds of years — he'd had to be cautious with the women he bedded. Humans were fragile. He had to hold back; he had to be careful not to hurt them. He could not forget his strength, could never entirely let go. He found release and so did his partners, but he had never been entirely free.

With her, he could be free. Linara had taken all he had to give. She had given just as strongly.

She was indeed Ksana. No ordinary man would've been able to survive fucking her. He wanted her again, and again, and again. He wanted to stay in this cave forever, with her.

That was a dangerous thought. He had not given up on his quest for a true mate. Another like him must exist somewhere in this world. A female dragon, a mate he could spend his life with. Humans, even demons, were temporary distractions, nothing more. Linara could only be his at the moment. A month, a year, twenty years or more...

Eventually, she would know who he was, though, and then what? Would she choose sex over her assassin's mission? How dedicated was she to her kind?

How dedicated was she to *him*?

Her eyes fluttered open and she turned her head to look at him. "I should sleep," she whispered, "but I want you again. I feel as if I will die without you." She rolled onto her side. Her breasts brushed his chest, her fingers caressed his cheek, and he was hard again. "I have never experienced any feeling so intensely." Her eyes met his. "Is this love?"

Such a naive and unnecessary question, one he answered immediately.

"No."

CHAPTER 9

Val walked for hours, wading through and walking around flowing, whispering waters. Her mother had hated the voices of the stream, but Val found them not to be too intrusive. Perhaps the life force of the cavern allowed her to pass without much interference because they recognized her purpose. She glanced into the stream to catch a glimpse of her reflection, and for the first time she saw the rainbows in her eyes.

The life force of the cavern did not disturb her because it was a part of her. It was in her soul, in her essence. The voices did not disturb her because they were, in many ways, her own.

By morning's light, Val and Kitty left the cavern by way of a waterfall that seemed to contain all the colors of the rainbow. She had no qualms about jumping; she did not hesitate. The water she'd waded through had spoken to her as she'd approached the exit, whispering, encouraging, guiding.

The water, the light, the whispering, they were a part of her as much as Kitty.

It might have been wise to toss Kitty ahead, rather than jumping with a sword in her hand, but she could not, would not, let Kitty go. She had no idea where Uryen might be, and Uryen wanted Kitty. Sword in hand, Val descended quickly. She fell, she knew she was falling, but she could almost swear she was being carried. The water embraced her, cradled her, dropping her safely into the pond below.

Soaking wet, Val climbed out of the pond with Kitty gripped in her right hand. The sun was warm and much welcomed. A war awaited. But first, Cyrus.

She would make sure he was all right and then she would send him home. There was no other logical choice, and a warrior must rely on logic. How could she ever trust that he was who he was? If Uryen could fool her once, she could do it again. Cyrus would always be in danger if he tried to remain with her.

For a brief moment she wondered if it had been Cyrus or Uryen who'd admitted that he liked her. She shook off the thought. It didn't matter. Did it?

Heavens, if Uryen could make herself appear as Cyrus, then she could appear as anyone! The demon daughters had varying degrees of skill and strength. Some were pure evil; others, she had heard, possessed some goodness. There were shifters and those with power over the elements. One, Val had heard, made wishes that came true. She didn't know what Uryen's powers might be, but there was the fire in her hair to consider, as well as the more disturbing ability to change her appearance.

Uryen might appear to be Val's own father or mother. Strangers along the way. Friends. Family. She could trust no one.

She'd always known she would have to do this warrior thing alone, but realizing that she would be forced to remain entirely on her own was startling and disturbing. She could trust no one…unless she killed Uryen.

That was a part of her destiny; she'd known that for a long time. Destined warrior or not, she'd never actually killed anyone. Realizing it was coming and actually seeing the face of a woman — no, demon — she'd have to kill were not the same.

I have killed, Kitty whispered. *I will help you.*

Those words were meant to be comforting, Val imagined, but they were not.

Linara stepped cautiously from the cave into the sunlight, wondering if Stasio's screams would instantly enter her mind as she left the dragonstone behind. She trailed her fingers along the wall as long as she could, but finally, the stone and its protection were behind her.

For a moment there was nothing, and then an angry voice whispered. "Don't disappoint me. I will make your *mother* pay in a thousand ways if you do."

Linara held her breath. Her heart skipped a

beat. She should have realized that her dreams of escaping, of staying here, were nothing more than fantasy.

Stasio had never before threatened Sophie Fyne Varden. He had not dared. He'd become desperate in her absence. What was happening below? How was the war proceeding?

She did not care.

Perhaps Stasio had picked up on her recent fond memories of life in the Varden household. She should never have allowed herself to remember the love she had known there; she should never have allowed him to see...

Though she had run away from the family who had taken her in, Sophie was Linara's mother in every way that counted. If Stasio had threatened that kind woman while he and Linara had been face to face, he would have been dead before he'd hit the ground. Was that why he'd waited until she was so far away?

Her indecision was gone. She'd chosen poorly when she'd aligned herself with Stasio and those demon daughters who called themselves her sisters. She'd been so caught up in wondering who she was and what her place in the world was meant to be, that she'd allowed herself to be led in the wrong direction.

She would break with them all; she would live her own life. With Pax?

Lying with a man had affected her brain

temporarily. There was no turning back, not now.

Pax stepped from the cave and into the sun to join her. He was more tempting than before, and her body tingled at the sight of him. That smile, wicked and charming and sexy, grabbed her heart. No, wait…that was not her heart. Her heart was not located between her legs.

He growled a word she did not understand, and then he added, "You're so damn beautiful."

"So are you," she said truthfully.

He wrapped his arms around her and pulled her close. "Forget the dragon. Stay here, with me. War is not for us, Linara. We will fuck and eat and dance. What else do we need?"

It was an amazing picture, one she could see too well in her imagination. One she did not dare to embrace. She wanted it, so much. And yet…

"We have no music. How are we to dance?"

"There is always music." He took her in his arms and spun her around. Fast, too fast. Then his steps slowed, and he hummed a tune she had never heard before. She rested her head on his chest, wrapped her arms around him, and together they moved in time with the slow tune. He was so warm and strong; he was everything she'd ever imagined a man might be.

She stopped in her tracks, and his tune ended. She made herself step away from him as she said, "Perhaps when my job here is done."

His smile faded. "After you kill the dragon."

She thought of her mother, her father, her brothers and sisters. Stasio would not be content with only Sophie. He would kill them all if she did not finish this mission. "Yes. Will you help me?"

"Probably not," he said. "Why do you want to kill the dragon, anyway? He keeps to himself, he stays on this mountain and does not interfere in the doings of humans below. He's killed a few of your kind, true, but they were demons intent on bringing harm to the people of these mountains so that seems only fair."

Linara took a deep breath and exhaled the words. "One born, one hatched, one created."

"Explain," Pax said simply.

She did.

Val retraced her steps. It was not an easy task, since she had to round the mountain and climb to the area where she had been, searching for an entrance to the cave. Cyrus had been wounded days ago. How many days? Two? Five? Had he bled to death while she'd been...

No. She would not allow that to be. A perfectly nice and ordinary boy who liked her, who called her friend, could not die simply because he'd decided to join her on her quest.

She repeated that silently, over and over, but a deeper part of herself was resigned. This was war. Anyone might be sacrificed.

Not Cyrus. Please, not him.

Kitty was annoyed with the delay. Val felt that annoyance. She gripped the sword and felt the power of it, the emotion, the thoughts, as if they were a part of her. She'd need to find a proper sheath for Kitty before she continued. For now, the sword remained in her hand.

Rocks on the other side of the hill were disturbed. They skipped and skittered. Val held Kitty ready, and stepped in that direction. Might be an animal. Might be Uryen. Then again, it could be...

"Cyrus!"

He came into view, and though she knew he had been wounded, the sight of the dried blood on his shirt and one side of his face alarmed her. She was instantly incensed. If Uryen showed herself now, Val would not hesitate to kill the demon.

"Thank the Gods!" Cyrus said, rushing toward her. He stumbled a little, and Val rushed to put her free arm around him. Just to steady him, of course. "I thought...I thought you might be dead, or gone. I looked everywhere..."

"It was Uryen," Val said. As soon as Cyrus was on firm footing again, she released him. Slowly. Kitty's energy stung her palm, a little. Her chin came up. "I am glad to see you well. I was afraid..." *I was afraid you were gone. I was afraid you were dead. I was afraid I would never see you again.* "I thought she might've killed you." Her words were almost without emotion.

Cyrus placed a cautious hand on the wounded side of his head. There was so much dried blood in his fair hair. Why hadn't he cleaned himself? How long ago, precisely, had he been attacked and replaced? How long had he been unconscious?

Val took a step away, narrowing her eyes to study the boy before her. Was this truly Cyrus? Was Uryen up to her tricks again?

Kitty sounded almost petty as she whispered, *It is he, weak human that he is.*

The reassurance of a magical sword was more comforting than she'd imagined it would be. Still, Val realized the best thing she could do for Cyrus was to send him home. And so, she tried to dismiss him.

He would not be dismissed so easily.

"You have to retrieve your horse in the village, so we might as well travel there together. Besides, I have something for you."

"What could you possibly have for me?" Val snapped.

Cyrus nodded toward Kitty. "I have made a sheath for your sword."

How was that possible? He could not know the proper size and shape; he could not know...

"I dreamed of that sheath for years, until the day came when I knew I had to fashion it myself," Cyrus explained. "It is made of the finest leather." He blushed, as if he were ashamed. "I engraved a V on one side. It's rather fancy. There are some swirls and flowers on the other. You didn't come, and it seemed silly to set the work aside without making it…special."

She did need her horse, and she had already thought of a sheath for Kitty. She just had not imagined that Cyrus might've made one for her. "Do you have magic?"

"Not to my knowledge."

"Then how can you be sure your creation will be sufficient?"

He smiled. Yes, this was indeed Cyrus. "There is only one way to find out."

Linara walked to the pond to bathe as she pondered her next steps. Much as she wanted to leave everything she knew behind to remain here on this mountain, that was no longer possible.

She dropped her shift on the rocks and stepped into the pond. It looked warm, but was not. The water was cold, much colder than she'd expected it to be. She trailed her fingers through the water as she stepped deeper and deeper, and wished it was warmer.

Instantly, it was. The once cold pond was now the perfect temperature for a bath, relaxing and soothing. Linara smiled as she dipped down so that the water touched her chin. Was this a sign that she was discovering her powers, or was it a power of the dragonstone that ran through the rock that created this pond?

She did not care.

It seemed clear that when she was under the protection of the dragonstone, Stasio could not touch her mind. Only here and in the cave could she allow herself to think of what she'd do to the wizard who had dared to threaten her mother. In short order she would end the dragon — or he would end her. If she survived, she'd return to the village where Stasio had gathered his army, and she would kill him. It would not be easy, but anyone, anything, could and did die.

She could spare the dragon, she supposed, and simply return to the village and kill the dark wizard. But if he saw, if he knew…Linara's mother would pay. If Linara slew the dragon, Stasio would never suspect her treachery. Sophie Fyne would be safe, and Stasio would not see his own death coming.

If she could discover and hone her powers, they might help her to do what had to be done. Destroy the dragon. Destroy Stasio.

And then?

She would go home, beg for forgiveness, and do everything possible to drive the demon half of herself out. Was that possible? Was there enough magic in the world to protect her, and those around her, from what she'd been born to be?

For a large man, Pax moved with amazing silence. It was a minor disturbance in the water that alerted her to his presence. She turned to watch him walk into the pond to join her.

"It is warmer than usual. Is that your doing?"

"I don't know."

His dark eyebrows lifted slightly.

"My powers have not yet manifested."

"You are of an age to know what gifts, or curses, you possess."

"An amulet protected me for some years. Now that I am without it…I wait."

"Wait for what?"

It was a good question, one that made her heart pound. "For the knowledge of what I might do with what I am."

Pax reached her, wrapped his arms around her, pulled her close. She reveled in the sensation of his skin against hers, wallowed in the closeness, the desire, the knowledge that he wanted her as much as she wanted him.

She could very well imagine simply staying here. Perhaps she could fashion something with the dragonstone, something she might wear, that would keep Stasio out of her mind forever. She wanted him out. She wanted him gone.

In Pax's arms, she could imagine a new life. A simple life. A wonderful life. At least, for a while she could pretend.

Without warning, he dipped beneath the water, dragging her with him, immersing them in the clear, warm water.

The light from the stone danced through the water, pale and bright tendrils dancing around them. Pax's long hair floated around him, framing his fierce and beautiful face. When he kissed her, she felt as if she were in another world, another universe. There was nothing in existence but the two of them and the light. Nothing but warmth and desire and peace.

She had never known true peace, not until this moment. She'd been floundering all her life, and now...she had him. He was here. He was hers.

Then he was inside her. She thought she'd need to breathe, but there was no water, no air, no need but the need for Pax. They were one, a part of this mountain and a part of one another. She climaxed almost instantly, and so did he. The colors encircling them changed, deepened, grew radiant and enchanting, and then, as Pax leaped up and out of the water, those colors faded.

She gasped for air; he laughed. She took his face in her hands and kissed him. Because she wanted it. Because she could. As he had last night, he fed her, with no ill effects to himself.

As her powers grew, would that change? Would the day come when she could not kiss him? That would be tragic, she decided as she took her mouth from his and placed her head on his shoulder.

"I'm glad I found you," she confessed.

"I am happy to be found."

"I wish I could stay here forever. If you would

have me, of course."

"Always, I would have you." There was a richness to his voice as he spoke those words.

"First I must kill the dragon."

Pax's eyes narrowed. "You would destroy him simply because you have been ordered to do so? He has done nothing to harm you."

She pressed her lips to his wet shoulder, and then she whispered, "I must."

He moved away from her, released her, and in his eyes she saw condemnation. Disappointment. He created a physical distance, backing away from her. "You must," he repeated. "You would choose death and destruction over this. You would choose war over us."

Linara turned around. She didn't want to look into those disappointed eyes. If she told him why she had no choice, would he care? Would he continue to help her? She did not rely on anyone other than herself. She did not share her worries, her pain, not with anyone. If she had, maybe she never would've run away from home. If she had not kept all her indecisions and agonies locked deep inside, the burden would have been lighter. Perhaps she could share with Pax, here and now.

"My mother," she said. "My family. He will..."

She turned around to face Pax, to try to explain, but he was already gone.

And the water went cold.

CHAPTER 10

The uncomfortable distance between them which Pax had created when he'd walked away remained, growing stronger throughout the day. Physically he stayed close, but the way he held his large body, the way he looked at her — the change was sharp and disconcerting.

She'd liked it so much better when he'd held her and asked her to stay, to dance, to live. As if such a life might ever be a choice for her. She could dream, she could fool herself for a while, but she knew her path in life had already been set, and it did not include Pax, love, or dancing.

Since she'd warmed the water on that morning, Linara decided to try again to discover what powers might manifest. Being away from the amulet for some time, being fed, and being free from Stasio and her own half-demon sisters, allowed a part of her that had been sleeping to wake. A little. She felt something new inside her, and when she imagined that what she felt was like the slivers of light in the dragonstone, she could control it.

She might need all her powers to kill the dragon.

All that day, and the next, and the next, Linara

worked to bring the new light inside her to life. It wasn't easy, but she worked hard and the light — light bright and dark — grew stronger. Once, as she stood a distance away from the cave where the stone was so powerful, Stasio crept into her mind. *Do not delay.*

She forced him out with a mental warning and erected a barrier so strong she felt him flinch before he disappeared.

Was it possible that he was out of her mind for good? If she prayed, she would pray it was so.

Barefoot on the cool stone, dressed only the white shift that she'd worn beneath her sturdier traveling gown — which was now much the worse for wear — she concentrated on her abilities, her spirit, and the essence of the stone that seemed to feed her much as her companion had. On occasion a breeze would whip around her, cool and strong, but she felt no pain in it, not even the slightest discomfort.

As she worked, Pax ignored her. Hadn't he said he would leave? He remained, and did not seem at all inclined to head down the mountain. She didn't ask him again to go. This was, after all, his home, not hers. That wasn't to say nothing had changed. When she went to the pond, she went alone. When she slept, he did not join her. He did not touch her. Now and then he wandered away without explanation, to hunt or perhaps just to get away from her. She missed him, she missed his touch, but she would not beg. Not for him or for anything else.

On the fourth day, all that she'd been working for seemed to click into place. She had worked a wooden puzzle once, and it was much like that, as one piece and then another fell together. The world shifted; the world was hers. She felt everything, in the air, in the stone, in the water. She felt, intensely, the life on this mountain. The Anwyn and Caradon. The animals. The trees. All aspects of this land filled her, intense and powerful, beautiful and fierce.

She lifted her hand and created a fire on her palm. With a thought, it extinguished as quickly as it had been born. She took a deep breath and exhaled, and a cool breeze whipped around her. Even in the distance, the trees swayed with that breath. The colors within her, the tendrils of power, spread out and grew.

Knowledge was hers; she saw so much. Her family was well, though danger crept near them. She frowned. The family was divided, but all were alive and well. She wished for details, but could see none. Her parents were never separated for long, but while they were currently safe, they were not together. Was that Stasio's doing? She could not be sure, but she suspected that was the case.

The world was at war, with pockets of peace as well as pockets of horror. Armies marched. Her demon sisters attacked.

The dragon flew.

For years, Stasio had invaded her mind without

invitation, without warning. He had nudged, cajoled, and threatened. Standing on this mountain she now thought of as hers, she pushed into his thoughts.

Threaten my family again, and I will gut you. I can do it from here.

She felt his response. The dark wizard was alarmed, and then he was pleased. Before she ended the connection he spoke to her with an annoying smugness.

Nice to finally meet you, Ksana.

The village was a welcomed sight. Finally! Val had a simple plan. She would collect her horse and the sheath Cyrus had made for Kitty, and then she'd move on. Even though it was late in the day, she wouldn't spend the night here, not with her relatives, and certainly not with Cyrus' family. She'd collect what she needed and ride away from the Village of the Turis to be alone again. It was time.

She would follow Kitty's lead and join the fight she was destined to lead. She wasn't sure where or how just yet, but something in her whispered *North*. She had heard that was where the fiercest battles had been fought in the past year, so it made some sense.

And what of Uryen? That was another reason to move on quickly. Val knew that if no one was with her, she would put no one's life in danger. Cyrus could've been killed. That was an unpleasant thought. He was a friend, after all. The only one she had!

Soldiers died in war, she knew that, but Cyrus was no soldier. He was a farmer's son, one who had *supposedly* prophetic dreams and worked with leather, but still, a farmer. He was strong, thanks to years of helping his father, and he was at least moderately intelligent. It had been nice to have him along as a companion, for a while. Still, he was *not* a soldier.

She did not want him to die.

Her friend did not ask her to stay, or wonder aloud if she would visit her family before moving on. He knew better. Cyrus left Val at his family's kitchen table with hot cider, oatcakes, and a bowl of hearty stew, while he slipped away to collect her horse. She didn't want to see her cousins, didn't want to be told that she needed to stay and wait for her father or — horrors — find out that he was already here, waiting for her.

Trust no one. Need no one. See this war won and then, maybe...

No, no maybes. Not yet.

Val thanked Cyrus' shy mother for the food. The woman kept her eyes lowered and clasped her hands, when those hands weren't busy with her womanly work. Was she always so shy or was she afraid of the warrior who'd just scarfed down a large meal in her home? Val was accustomed to people looking at her as if she were strange, avoiding her at all costs, acting as if by being in her presence they, too, might be called upon to fight.

She wasted no time or words trying to break through Mistress Bannan's fear. Sincere thanks delivered, Val walked out of the rear door. A large garden, much of it newly planted, grew close by. There were early vegetables that could withstand the cool nights, as well as many new plants that would be bursting with produce come summer. Beyond there were fields where Cyrus' father and brothers worked. It was a nice sight, pleasant, green, and peaceful. She soaked the sight in, as she knew there was not much in the way of peace before her.

Only minutes passed before Cyrus rounded the corner of the house, leading the mare Val had left with her cousins. She was relieved and afraid, ready and reticent.

Her time had come.

She took the reins and patted Snowflake on the neck. "I hope my kin gave you no trouble."

Cyrus blushed a little. "I saw no one. I thought it best to quietly…"

"Steal my horse for me," Val finished when he faltered.

He smiled. The blush faded. "Yes. I thought that would be best."

He had been hiding the sheath he'd made for Kitty behind his back, and he whipped it out with some small fanfare. It was indeed beautiful, though she hesitated in telling him so. She did not need beauty; she needed things — and people — with purpose.

But the V he had worked into the leather was special, she'd admit. Even the flowers on the other side were unexpectedly detailed and elegant. His work was fine, perfectly fashioned, without flaw. She took the offered sheath, immediately running one hand along the soft leather to show her appreciation. She asked Cyrus to hold Kitty while she strapped on the thin belt that was attached. Neither of them, not the friend or the weapon, cared for the arrangement.

As soon as the belt and sheath were properly positioned, she took Kitty from Cyrus and slipped the blade into its place. It was a perfect fit.

She felt a real and true warrior, now, with the promised sword, a proper sheath, and Snowflake. Her time had come. Finally!

A part of her wanted to close the short distance that separated them, go up on her toes, and kiss Cyrus' mouth. Nothing romantic, or anything, just a thanks.

Of course, she had not kissed his mother in thanks for the food.

"Thank you for your assistance, and for the fine scabbard," she said in a firm voice. Her tone was that of a soldier, not a woman. Or a girl. "I'm sorry you were injured."

He lifted an easy hand to the side of his head,

which they had wisely cleaned well before Cyrus' mother could see the evidence of his injury. "It was nothing."

No, it was something, but she didn't dare extend the conversation. She nodded once and started walking, leading her horse through a field so she could reach the road without being seen.

She had not gone far when Cyrus called out, "I can come with you."

Val stopped, turned, and looked at him. He was disturbingly handsome. "No. But thank you for the offer," she added, a bit belatedly. She turned from him once more, and this time when he spoke to her, telling her that she should not do this alone, she ignored him. Something must've flown into her eyes, dust or pollen perhaps, because she teared up a little.

She reached the road, glanced in both directions to make sure she was alone, and mounted her horse. And as she rode away, she wondered if she'd ever see Cyrus Bannan again.

Linara had changed in the days she'd spent honing her skills. With every passing hour, she became more confident, surer of herself. Pax watched from a distance. He growled. He'd liked her better when she'd been a simple girl intent on killing him.

At the moment she was a powerful demon, still

intent on killing him.

She did not know he was the dragon. How could she? So why did he feel betrayed that she had not given up her quest? Why was he angry that she wouldn't leave behind all that she knew — war, magic, missions — for him?

Pax had not given up on his quest for a mate, but it might be many more years before he found that for which he searched. He would continue with his life until that time; he would know pleasure and purpose. For a short while, he had thought Linara could be a part of that pleasure and purpose. He had chosen her.

She had not chosen him.

Night fell, and he continued to watch. By night the colors of her soul were more distinct than they were by daylight. Brighter, more vivid, easier to discern. She had always had some black in her aura, but that black had been muted by the other colors of the rainbow. Colors that represented goodness, compassion, even love. The full moon seemed to emphasize the brightness and the darkness of her.

She had taken to wearing nothing but a loose, white underthing, a simple dress of sorts, that allowed her complete freedom of movement. She had set her boots aside days ago, and was always barefoot. If she was bothered by the cold that lingered here at the top of the world, she did not allow it to show. She seemed to like the feel of stone against the soles of her feet. He suspected she had found a connection to the earth, with her feet against the stone of this mountain.

As she made a small pile of broken dragonstone dance around her, the love in her all but disappeared. The black grew. Some of the other colors darkened as well. His heart fell. His heart should have nothing to do with her.

He should kill her now. Tonight. Before she became so powerful that she could not be killed. He could take his dragon form and cook her, as he had cooked the others like her, or he could take her head with his sword. She would not see the threat coming; she believed him to be caught in her spell. By the time she realized his intent it would be too late.

But he remained where he was, watching.

He had never before been conflicted. An uncertain dragon. That was a disturbing thought.

The stones Linara had been manipulating were guided to the ground, where they clinked together musically as they came to rest. When that was done, Linara looked at him. He'd only thought he was hidden in this stand of trees. She'd realized all along that he was there. That he watched. Did she have any idea what he'd been thinking?

A new trick: She snapped her fingers, and a fire leaped to life on the pile of small rocks. It was an entrancing and colorful fire, and she was beautiful in the light that fire cast around the clearing.

"Did you bring supper?" she asked.

Pax moved forward, and as he stepped into the circle of light he lifted the three small animals carried in his right hand. "Two *tilsi* and a piglet."

"That will do nicely. I'm starving."

Starving? Not for game, he suspected. "I'm sure training yourself to be an evil power works up quite an appetite."

He saw the anger in her, the ire, the possibility of violence. And then those all faded, and he saw in her acceptance. "It does. And you know full well that I need more than *tilsi* and pork."

"Am I to feed myself with the meat so you can feed on me?"

And now, sadness. "Yes."

"If I refuse?"

She could take what he refused to give; she was that strong. Or soon would be.

"Then I will leave. I will trek down this mountain until I find another man and take from him what you will not give me."

Dangerous as she was, he did not want her to kiss another man, much less...

"If your touch weakens me will you stop, as you offered to do in the past?"

"If I can," she whispered.

If she was too far gone she would've lied to him, but she told the truth. She had always told him the truth.

He wondered when the time would come that he would do the same.

CHAPTER 11

Pax ate well. Linara picked at a bit of over-cooked *tilsi*, but that wasn't what she wanted or needed.

If she kissed Pax and her feeding drained him, would she stop before taking it all? Could she? She was much more powerful now than she had been the last time they'd touched. It had been days, and she was starving.

Awakening the demon inside her was hungry business.

They did not bother to go into the cave tonight. The weather was neither cold nor hot. The full moon shone bright, and so did her dragonstone fire.

Pax removed his kilt and the ragged shirt. Linara admired him for a moment. She had never known a man like this one, so rough and yet pleasing to the eye, so strong and powerful. Those dark, slightly slanted eyes had the power to look right through her. His hair, so full and dark and long, made him appear to be as much beast as man. It would be a shame to remove him from the world.

"I will stop, if you ask," she said as she removed her shift. She wore nothing over or under that simple garment.

They met in the center of the clearing, away from the fire. She could douse that fire, or reduce the flame, but she did not. She wanted to see him by moonlight and firelight. She wanted to savor him and all that they had together, while she could. It would not last much longer.

She did not kiss his mouth; not yet. Instead, she placed her lips on his chest. He was hard and warm. She could feel his heartbeat, which was strong and steady and a bit slower than she'd thought it might be. Even this gentle contact fed her, in some way she could not describe.

In his arms, she was not alone. With his body pressed against hers she was stronger. She was not Linara or Ksana; she was both. She was who she'd been born to be. Powerful. Hungry. Connected to this world to its core. To her core.

She lifted her face to his, wondering if she dared yet to kiss him. He did not lower his mouth to hers, so she, too, waited. They dropped gently to the ground; Pax shifted onto his back and pulled her atop him. Chest to chest, she straddled him. He was hard, and so close. She was wet, and she throbbed for him. They were together, but soon they would be more. They would be one.

Was she poison to him now that she had found her strength? She would soon find out.

Linara lowered her head slowly and kissed the man beneath her. Softly at first, tentatively. She would withdraw if her touch harmed him, she swore it. As much as it would hurt, she would move away from him before he was inside her.

As it had before, his kiss fed her. She was instantly stronger; her hunger faded. She forced herself to take her lips away, to look into his dark eyes. He did not seem to be affected in a negative way, but how could she be sure?

"Don't stop," he whispered, his voice as steady and strong as ever. "You are afraid you'll kill me with your body. I am afraid I will die if you take it away."

And then he was inside her, and everything went away but the way he made her feel. She did not think about feeding; she did not think about war or powers or demons or soldiers or dragons. She only thought about Pax. She needed him. She didn't need anything else.

She lifted up and then dropped to take him all, to sway in time with his slow heartbeat, to rise up and slide down and savor every sensation. This was beauty. This was power.

They moved faster, in time, in a frantic dance. She climaxed with a scream that reverberated all around her, in the stone and the trees, in the pond below, into the sky. Pax was with her, and she opened her eyes to watch him, to see his face as he gave in to this pleasure.

His eyes were closed, but he opened them to look into her face.

Those eyes glowed red and yellow, orange and

black. They looked into and through her, they held her captive.

She knew those eyes.

Pax was the dragon.

Linara scrambled away from him. She had seen the truth, in his most vulnerable moment, and now she was afraid. She, who should know no fear.

"You...you..."

"I am the one you seek, yes," Pax said as he stood.

"How?" she whispered.

He wondered if she would come to her senses and try to kill him now, while he was in his more vulnerable human form. She did not look at all dangerous at the moment, sitting naked on the stone, her silver hair draped around her as she stared at him.

"I will explain later, if you will listen," he said. "Danger is coming. Your scream as I pleasured you has drawn it to us."

She calmed herself and glanced into the woods. "Animals," she whispered.

"Caradon," he clarified, and then he looked at the full moon. "They usually travel alone, but I sense..." He closed his eyes and took a deep breath. "A pack." He frowned.

She knew what he was, so he did not step away to shift. There was pain, there always was, as his body grew and changed, as he left the man behind and became his true self. The moon grew brighter to his sensitive eyes, and so did she. So many colors, so much pain and confusion. So much love. He scratched at the stone with one talon and whipped his tail behind him, taking out a tree at the edge of the wood. He lifted his head to the night sky, took a long, deep, hot breath.

Then he shifted his head to look at her again. He towered over Linara and watched as she scooted away from him. She seemed so small now, so insignificant. He leaned down and sniffed, smelling her, watching the essence of her. She tried so hard to be powerful and dark, but while there was more darkness within her than there had been when he'd first seen her, she was not yet evil.

Pax saw her passion for him within her. Her fear of him, her admiration. A single breath, and she would be charred beyond recognition. He could fly away and the pack of Caradon would feed on what was left of her.

It would be the simplest way to end this.

Pax spread his wings and flew up. Linara grew smaller and smaller as the distance between them grew. She still sat there, naked and vulnerable, cowering against the stone wall. Were those tears on her face? Were they tears of sorrow or fear?

She was so intent upon him that she did not sense the Caradon — eight of them — until they were in the clearing and springing toward her, claws extended. He did not have to kill her. The shapeshifting beasts would gladly do the job for him.

Pax did what dragons do. He spat fire into the clearing to destroy his enemies.

Linara watched the flame swirling from above, as the fierce cat-like creatures ran toward her. They screamed, the fire roared, her heart pounded so hard that she could hear it above all the rest.

This was how it would end. She would not destroy the dragon, he would destroy her. Maybe Stasio would leave her family alone, after she was gone. Maybe there was a place in the Land of the Dead for her. She closed her eyes and waited to be consumed by the fire.

The Caradon screamed, piercing, unnatural screams that made her brain hurt. She felt heat, but no pain.

Linara opened her eyes. Fire blazed all around, but it did not touch her. The attacking animals burned. They screamed and writhed and six of them, the closest six, died. Two of the beasts were in the back of what had been a powerful and dangerous pack, away from the semi-circle of fire that now protected her. They both screamed, then growled, and then turned and ran.

The dragon gave chase, leaving Linara alone.

Suddenly all was quiet, but for her heart. For a

moment she sat there, trying to grip the stone beneath her, trying to melt into the stone wall behind. Pax had not killed her; he had saved her. Those animals could have ripped her apart in her stunned and unprepared state. She might have survived, if they had left her head attached to her body and some of her heart had escaped destruction, but she could've been badly wounded. It might have taken years to recover.

If they had eaten her...

Her newfound powers had done her no good at all when danger had come. She'd not been prepared. Could one ever be prepared for such an attack? Love one moment; violence the next. If not for Pax, she would not have survived.

Long after the Caradon and the dragon — Pax — had gone, the fire continued to burn. It was dragonfire, after all, and was somehow much like the stone in and around the cave. Eventually, it waned, and she could see beyond the protective flames.

The Caradon were not just dead; there was nothing left of them but dust and a bit of bone. The charred bone continued to smoke a little. She stood, her knees shaky. That could have been her.

That should have been her.

Anger rose up inside her. When danger had come she'd frozen, she'd panicked. She had been a worthless human, not a powerful daughter of the Isen Demon.

Linara leaped over a low spot in the ring of fire and grabbed her shift. She pulled it on as she made her way to the cave to collect what she had.

Inside the cave, she did not have to worry about Stasio peeking into her mind, thanks to the enchanted stone that surrounded her. She had more control over her thoughts than she'd ever had, but once she left this place, she would be vulnerable. Stasio might peek into her mind if she let her guard down.

She could not let him.

Linara pulled her dress on over her shift, and stepped into her boots. When she'd started her journey the gown had been sturdy, even pretty, as had the boots. Both were worn now, but they would suffice for a while longer. She didn't suppose what she wore mattered at all. She checked her sack, made sure there was water in the skin she carried. She wasn't well-armed, but she had her knives, and she needed nothing else. With her newly found powers, she didn't even need the knives, not really.

And yet…the sword, Pax's sword, caught her eye. Barely thinking, she grabbed it, testing the weight, swinging the heavy weapon to see if she could. The grip was too large for her hand, but she could manage.

She left the cave, sword in hand, and stepped quickly to the fire she'd built earlier. The flames had died when the much greater fire from the dragon had burst into the clearing. She reached down and scooped up a handful of rocks, and then another. Pieces of hot dragonstone filled her pockets. The stone increased her power. She didn't know why, but the why didn't matter.

The moon lit her way as she began to travel down the mountain. She was strong tonight, thanks to Pax. She was *alive*, thanks to Pax. She would not kill him, no matter what the consequences might be.

How could she save her family without fulfilling her mission?

There was only one way.

Stasio had to die.

CHAPTER 12

The two surviving Caradon parted ways not long after escaping the crispy slaughter of the other six of their pack. Pax chased down the larger of the two, watching its path through the trees, smelling and sensing it. There was no way to hide from a dragon's eye. The moment the cat leaped into a clearing, Pax sent his fire swirling and the cat met the same fate as the others. It burned and died screaming.

It could not live to attack Linara again.

That left one. If the single surviving Caradon was allowed to live, it would try to exact revenge. It would be best to end it tonight, before the shifter had the chance to gather reinforcements. Pax flew until sunrise, searching for that cat, but the creature had gone to ground. It was in a cave, or underground so deep that there was no way to find it. Yet. Wherever it had gone, it was well hidden. There was no scent, no sound, no hint of a shifter's energy.

He should've allowed the Caradon to end Linara. They'd save him the trouble of killing her himself.

Who was he kidding? He could not kill her, not

even to save his own life. He could not, would not, allow anyone or anything else to harm her, either.

As the sun came up and the sky turned orange, Pax flew to the clearing where he'd left Linara. Knowing his secret, would she try to kill him now? That was her mission, after all, her reason for being here. Would he let her?

He knew as his talons touched the ground that she had gone. She was not in the cave or at the pond. She'd fled this place hours ago. Only the faintest of her scent remained here.

She'd be easy enough to find, if he were so inclined. Was he? Should he let her go?

He shifted into his human form once more, and stepped into the cave where he had first lain with Linara. Where he had kissed her. Where he had surprised her by his survival. It would be better to cut all ties, to release her. He wouldn't have to kill her, and she wouldn't kill him. They could go their separate ways, war or no war.

That was for the best, but it did make him sad. He'd miss her, his sexy half-demon assassin. He'd miss watching her, kissing her. He would definitely miss the sex. But still…it was for the best.

He would sleep today; he needed his rest. Tonight he would hunt the one remaining Caradon of the pack that had attacked his home and Linara. Would that shifter come after him or track Linara? Would he gather reinforcements or try to finish the job on his own? The shifter would be in for a surprise If he thought he was hunting a weak woman. Last night she'd been surprised, first by him and then by the attack. She would not be taken unaware again, and she would not be passive, as she had been last night.

Even though it was for the best, he longed for her already. He did not want to let her go.

As Pax settled on a fur rug to sleep, he rolled to the side and glanced into the far corner. After a moment his heart lightened, and he grinned. Linara had taken his sword. No matter what the circumstances might be, no matter what was best, he had to go after her and retrieve it.

Val had been riding for two days, following her instincts and Kitty's direction. The sword did speak to her, but still, her travels were lonely. She missed Cyrus.

He is behind us, you know, Kitty whispered.

"I know."

I can wound him so he won't be able to continue.

"You will not!"

Just a small wound, Kitty said contritely. *A minor...*

"No."

Kitty sighed. What an annoying habit in a sword!

"He's a nice boy, and well-intentioned."

He's a pain in the ass and he'll get you killed.
"Ridiculous."
All too possible.
They were headed north, as Val had known she would when the time came. Jagged mountains much more majestic than those she'd left behind awaited in the distance.

She had no idea what would happen when she arrived there.

One behind and one ahead, Kitty whispered. *One is real and one is not. This time, I do not know which is genuine and which is demon. She has cast a spell to confuse me.*

"What are you talking about?" Val snapped, and then she saw him, directly in her path. Sitting his horse so straight and tall, as he always had. Sword at his side. Scowl on his face. His hair was much like hers, curly and occasionally unruly. He had a few strands of gray now. Gray he unfairly blamed on her.

She did not speed up or slow down, but approached with some caution. When she was almost upon him she nodded and said, "Father. I imagined I would see you at some point on this journey."

He said nothing, but his expression spoke volumes.

Was this her father, the intimidating General Merin? Or was it Uryen wearing his skin?

Val stopped and dismounted.

"I'm going with you," her father said. Snapped, really, as he sometimes did when he was unhappy.

She looked closely at the face she knew so well, wishing she were closer so she could study every detail. As if it was possible there might be a flaw, whether this was her father or not.

"It's not necessary that you…"

"I'm not leaving."

Of course not. Neither her father nor the demon who wished to separate her from Kitty would ride away, no matter what she said.

"I'm going to rest here for a while," Val said.

"You won't change my mind," her father said as he dismounted.

"I am aware. You never change your mind." She hitched Snowflake to a low limb of a nearby tree. "I need to wait here for a while, in any case. A companion is a short way behind. I need to allow him to catch up."

Her father's eyebrows arched. "A companion?"

"A friend," she clarified. "Cyrus Bannan."

Her father seemed to snort at the mention of the boy's name, as fathers were wont to do.

Val stretched her legs and walked about, asking — as she should — about her mother and her siblings. The man before her offered short, insufficient answers. That in itself was not evidence, since that was General Merin's way.

Soon enough Cyrus would catch up with them, and they'd be a party of three. Val, either a friend or a father, and a demon wearing the face of someone she cared deeply about. How was she to discern which was Uryen if even Kitty couldn't tell?

No one had warned her being a warrior would be so emotionally distressing.

Linara walked with purpose, running when the landscape allowed. Over stone paths and into the woods. Out of the woods and onto rock again. When the path was steep she had to take care, but she moved as quickly as she could. It was difficult with her pack and the sword that was too large for her, but she managed. She needed to get as far away from Pax as she possibly could.

As if he couldn't flap his wings twice and travel from one end of the mountain to the other.

Maybe he wouldn't follow. Maybe he was glad to see her go.

His sword was heavy, but she was stronger than she'd been when she'd traveled up this mountain so she did not consider it to be a burden.

She didn't need the sword to take a life and Pax wouldn't need it to kill her, if he decided to do so. None of her Ksana sisters bothered with weapons. Why should they? She wasn't sure why she'd taken the sword, but she had. It was hers now, a token of remembrance from the man — dragon — beast — she had come to...

Well, not love. Not that. The beast she had come

to want, to need. To crave.

She'd been traveling as fast as possible and still at a pace that was agonizingly slow. The terrain was difficult. She kept the shields in her mind strong, as she thought of making her way to Stasio and killing him before he could hurt her mother. If he knew, if he even suspected...

Almost the entire day had passed and the sun was low in the sky when she heard the man coming. She even smelled him, with her newly awakened powers. He was a man, but he also had the odor of the cats who had attacked last night. Caradon. Shifter. There were many shifters in these mountains. Was he one of those who had tried to kill her, or was he an innocent?

Was any man truly innocent?

She rounded a corner in the path and stopped, slipping Pax's sword into a crevice between two rocks. Best if the creature coming thought her to be unarmed and helpless.

Linara had never been helpless, and now? No man or beast could harm her, as long as she accepted her powers and used them when necessary. Last night's failure could not be repeated.

She stepped to the edge of the path she'd been walking and looked out over the land that was so wild, so majestic. Maybe when the war was over she'd return here, live here, hide from the rest of the world and the truth of what she was. With Pax?

Of course not. He would hate her now. She'd

come to kill him, and he knew it. He'd murdered several of her kind, and would kill her if he got the chance.

Maybe. He'd had the chance just last night...

The scent of the creature grew stronger as he came near, but it was more than his smell that alerted her. She sensed the essence of him in a way that was new to her. Yes, he was one of those who had attacked last night. She'd not given much thought as to why the pack had attacked, but she pondered it now. The Caradon usually traveled alone on those nights when the moon was full and they were in their feline form. The Anwyn, wolf shifters like Aunt Juliet and most of her family, almost always traveled in a pack no matter what form they took. But the cats hunted alone.

What had brought the Caradon together to attack? Fear? Anger? A mission, perhaps.

She did not know how many creatures Stasio had influenced. Did the Caradon attacker work for him?

She had no answers, and there was no more time to ponder. The man who'd been tracking her arrived, and he claimed all her attention. He walked around a boulder and stopped suddenly, as if surprised to see her there. He was not truly surprised; his instincts were too keen for that.

Linara could pretend to be surprised, too. "Oh, my," she said breathlessly, as she had heard young women speak in the past. "You startled me. I thought I was alone on this trail."

The tall, solidly-built man had long, tangled dark hair and piercing green eyes. His nose was a bit sharp, and he had thin lips that attempted an insincere smile. "It is strange to run into another traveler here. Are you lost?"

Men! Pax had asked the same question. Best to allow this one to think she was incompetent. "Yes, I am."

He didn't believe her, not that that mattered. "You've run away, haven't you?"

More than once...

He was still tense, very much on alert. Best to play the helpless female a while longer. It was like a silly play. She knew he was lying, and he knew she was not lost. And yet, they each played their part, waiting for the right time to make a move. What did he want? Why had he not simply attacked? "My husband was not a good man. I left the farm as he slept and ran blindly." She clasped her hands. "I should have had a plan, I suppose. I did think there would be people here, someone who might help me."

He walked toward her, his eyes narrowed and suspicious. "My name is Naal. I will escort you to a village at the foot of the mountain, if you'd like."

"That's kind of you. My name is Linny." Close enough. Some of her nieces and nephews had called her Linny when they'd been small, and their tongues had had difficulty with Linara.

She could fetch Pax's sword and quickly take this man's head. She could take his face in her hands and kiss him, draining him of life. But she wanted to know why he and the others had attacked last night. Had they been looking for her or Pax? Did they realize he was the dragon?

Had Stasio sent the Caradon to do what she could not?

"Do you mind if we rest here a little while?" She gave a little smile. "My legs ache, and I'm a bit out of breath."

He answered with a casual bow, nodding his head and briefly sticking out one booted foot. "As you wish, Mistress Linny."

She sat on the edge of the path, so her feet dangled over the ledge. The view remained amazing, even though she was distracted by the presence of the beast who had tried to kill her last night. Hills green and granite stretched seemingly forever. In those hills there was no war. She could live here and with some care might never see another human being.

Without a man to feed upon, would she eventually die? Or would she just be forever weak and hungry?

Naal sat beside her, close but not too close. How fast was he? Did it matter that he was not disturbingly near?

"Did he beat you?" the Caradon asked, after they'd been resting a few minutes. When she did not immediately answer, he added, "Your husband, the one you ran from, did he beat you?"

It seemed a good enough reason for her to run from her fictional spouse. "Yes." She had heard tales of men who beat their women, had even seen a swordsman in the village take his fists to a woman who had displeased him. But the men she had known — her father, her brothers, Pax — would never be so cruel. They used their strength to protect, not hurt.

Well, Pax had cooked a demon or two, but...

Naal did not allow her to look at the land before them and contemplate the kindness of the men in her life. "If I had a wife as pretty as you, I would beat her often."

Linara turned her head to look at him, certain she must've misheard. She had not. "Why?"

"To remind her of her place. To make sure she never forgot that I was her master in all ways."

No man would ever be her master. She thought of Stasio and added, to herself, *never again*. "Wives do not care to have a master. They wish instead for a partner. A companion."

Naal scoffed, then whispered beneath his breath, "Stupid."

Even though he was not in his feline form, he was quick. He leaped from his seated position and grabbed Linara, pushing her onto her back, pressing her into the stone. Her feet dangled over the side of the mountain as he straddled her and, with a hand on her throat, held her motionless.

Had he come for her? Did he know how to kill a daughter of the Isen Demon?

He dispelled her worries with a question. "Where is he? The dragon, where does he sleep?"

"I... I..."

"Don't tell me you don't know. You stink of him."

Naal did not realize how strong she was, how dangerous she could be. He was looking for Pax, for the dragon, not for her.

"Why do you want to find him?"

The hand at her throat tightened. "That's none of your business."

"If I'm going to tell you where he sleeps, you must tell me why. Are you going to kill him?"

"Yes. My friends and I were promised a lot of gold if we would take the dragon's head."

"Promised by who?"

"A man you never want to meet," Naal whispered.

Stasio. She was sure of it.

His hand tightened again. "I can take his head when I find him. It will be easier if he's in his human form, but I will take him on no matter what shape he wears."

Naal knew the dragon he sought was a shifter. He knew the man who walked by day and the dragon who flew the night sky were one and the same. Did Stasio know? Had he known all along?

Why hadn't he told her?

She reached inside and calmed her heart and her breath. Stasio must not have told Naal and his friends what *she* was. If he knew, he would not remain so close to her.

"I can take you there," she said calmly.

"Just tell me where he is."

"You'll kill me," she whispered, injecting fear into her voice. "If you don't need me anymore, you'll kill me here and now, I know it."

"Maybe," he admitted.

Linara felt the power growing inside her. She hoped it did not show, not to Naal. "I don't want to die." It was true, and surprising in some ways. She'd never thought much about her future, about what good the days to come might bring. She had Pax to thank for that.

Naal smiled. It was not pleasant, not at all. "You can probably find a way to convince me of your worth." His hand wrapped around her neck and held her firmly. His head lowered slowly toward hers.

"You don't want to do this," she warned.

"Ah, but I do." His mouth was almost on hers. There was nothing pleasant about the possibility of a kiss from the Caradon. His breath was hot and sour, his lips thin and dry. And still, Linara's hunger came to life.

Again, she tried to warn him. "Stop."

Linara's entire body trembled. Naal likely thought she shook with desire in spite of her words of warning, that she was so weak and spineless that she would want a man who'd threaten her this way. It was not desire or fear that made her shake.

The longer he touched her, the closer his lips came to hers, the hungrier she became. That hunger grew inside her, stronger, more and more demanding. She did need him, but not in the way he imagined.

"If you kiss me you will know..."

He did not allow her to finish the sentence, but pressed his thin lips to hers.

The effect was immediate. Life and power flowed through her. Naal had to feel the drain on his life, had to know — too late — what she was. But he could not move, he could not save himself. They were drawn together, latched to one another. She was a parasite, and he fed her.

After fighting to block her thoughts from the wizard who had sent her to this mountain, Linara opened her mind to Stasio. She invaded his thoughts as he had so often invaded hers. *See me. See what you have made me.*

She was able to manipulate the images in her mind to tell Stasio the story she wished him to see. In her mind, the man who fed her was not Naal; it was Pax. She showed Stasio the amazing vision of Pax's transformation.

You told me I would find a way, and I did.

She knew it was not Pax above her, but the image she created in her mind was so real, tears slipped from her eyes. Those eyes burned, her heart ached.

Stasio would see that, too; he would feel her pain and rejoice in it.

Linara threw off what was left of Naal. He maintained a human shape for a moment, and then there were bones and clothing and dust. Nothing more. She scooted back, jumped to her feet, and vigorously brushed away the remnants of the attacker that clung to her clothing. The tears continued to fall, running along her dusty cheeks, burning.

I knew you could do this, Stasio whispered. *Now, it is time to come home. Come home to me.*

Linara shut down the connection without responding. A new fury grew in her heart, and it had to remain hidden from the wizard, for now. When she saw Stasio again, she would feed on him as she had just fed on Naal. She could not allow him to see her hatred for him and all he had done. Not yet.

Fed and powerful, her abilities still growing, Linara briefly reached out to her sisters, to the others who were touched with the evil that had been their father. Some were completely lost to darkness. Others, like her, struggled. There was more dark than light, but the light lived. Her sisters were in many ways like any other living being. They were good and bad. Some fought while others hid from the war, from what they were.

Battles raged in many souls, as it raged in hers.

Some, a lucky few, had had the darkness taken from them by a witch. Stasio had hidden the knowledge of the witch from her; he had kept close the fact that the demon could be stripped away for some. She saw it, in vague images and streaks of energy, in dancing colors that reminded her of the dragonstone. Looking out upon the world, Linara roused a name and an image. *Lyssa.* Stasio wanted to end that witch's life; he'd been trying to do so, unsuccessfully, for a long while.

Could that witch help her? Could even the first Ksana be...healed? It was too much to hope for, and yet she did hope. Before she met this remarkable witch, she needed to find Pax and warn him to move north, to hide himself from eyes that believed him to be dead.

Linara collected his sword and began to retrace her steps, sparing Naal no more than a glance. She should continue to the south. She wanted to end Stasio. Was the threat to her mother immediate, or was it as empty as Stasio's soul? Wouldn't she feel it if the danger was close?

As for Lyssa...when she found the witch, would she use her? Would she willingly give up the strongest part of herself? This Lyssa could save her from the demon, but with power flowing through her as it was at this moment, Linara wasn't entirely sure she wanted to be saved. The battle inside her continued. Still, she walked on, back toward the dragon's lair.

Why did she care about saving Pax? What difference did it make to her if he lived or died?

Love, a voice within her whispered.

She shook off that ridiculous word and once again walked north.

CHAPTER 13

Sitting by the campfire, Val looked at her father and then at Cyrus, and then back again. For hours she'd been trying to determine which was genuine and which was Uryen in another's form. She should be sleeping, she should rest for the day ahead, but how could she sleep knowing one of her companions was an impostor but not being able to tell which one?

Her father acted like her father. He was angry that she'd run away and determined to protect her. It didn't help that he had always been stoic. Perhaps if he'd been a talkative man she'd have been able to catch him in a mistake. Instead, he mostly glared and scowled. And occasionally growled. Typical. She tried to think of a question that might trip up a phony, but nothing seemed quite right. General Tearlach Merin was well known in Columbyana. It would not have been difficult for Uryen to study the details of his life, both public and private.

Cyrus was, well, Cyrus. He was sheepish on occasion, and was openly intimidated by the great General Merin. He seemed genuine enough, but Uryen had fooled her before where the farmer's son was concerned.

When the demon took on the form of another, did she take on anything more than simple form? Perhaps she knew their thoughts, or took on their true personalities. How was she to know?

Kitty was no help at all. She could sense Uryen was present, but could not tell which man was the demon in disguise. They were all under some spell of confusion, cast by the demon.

Why had Uryen not attacked yet? The demon wanted the sword, that much was clear, and she had powers of some sort that might help her when it came time to attack two humans, whether those two were a young warrior and her much more experienced father, or a young warrior and a farmer's son. So, why the delay?

Afraid.

"Afraid of what?" Val whispered.

Afraid of you. And me.

"Well, what's she waiting for?"

The right time.

"There have been opportunities for her to…you know."

She doesn't just want to kill you; she wants to be you. She wants to control me, wear your face, and lead the men you are destined to command into a war they cannot win.

Val's heart almost stopped. She could see that scenario too well, and it was a horror. "I can't allow that to happen."

Val pursed her lips when both her father and

Cyrus looked at her as if she might be talking to them, even though she kept her voice very low. They didn't ask for clarification, though. If her father was her father, he would know of all the sword's powers. She hadn't told Cyrus the sword spoke to her and she talked back, but he'd probably figured it out by now. He was, on occasion, astute.

Again she asked, "What's she waiting for?"

Kitty was silent for a moment, as if searching for the answer. Finally, she said, her voice trembling, *She waits for her demon sisters. I do not know why.*

Val was exhausted, and dawn would be here soon. How could she sleep when a demon who wanted her dead was in her camp?

I do not sleep. I will wake you if you are needed.

Great. The only being in her camp she could trust was a thing.

Not just a thing, Kitty responded, even though Val had not spoken aloud. *I am more than a thing. I have a soul. I have a purpose. I was created for you.*

A chill walked up Val's spine.

She did not want to say the words aloud, so again she thought, *Are you the promised one created?*

Kitty did not answer, not as she had in the past, but she did vibrate at a new level. She hummed. She sang.

One created…

***

Pax soared over the mountain, staying closer to the ground than he normally did. He moved fast; his long body slithered and his tail whipped. Over trees, around ridges, he flew. He'd slept too long, then he'd lingered at the campsite a while, pondering what he'd do when he found Linara. There was no rush to begin his search. He would find her, no matter where she tried to hide.

He'd not been looking for her long, even though it was well past midnight. He could smell Linara on the path, in the trees, in the very stone. He smelled her so keenly he had no doubt that he could find her in any corner of the world.

She'd come to his home to kill him, but she had not. Not yet. She had the blood of a demon inside her, could kill an ordinary man with a kiss, could manipulate water and stone and gods only knew what else. If anyone could take his life, it was she.

She had stolen his sword. Had she known that would send him after her? Was that part of her plan?

Demon. Assassin. Thief.

And his. To the pit of his soul, Linara was his.

He could sense that the single surviving Caradon he also sought had been along this trail hours earlier. In search of Linara? Perhaps. His first thought was that she could defend herself since she had his sword. His second was that she did not need his sword to kill.

The path he followed in his search skirted the edge of the mountain. He flew dangerously close to two tall and jagged rock walls where there was a cave too small for him when he was in his natural state. He'd slept there a time or two as a man. He knew every crevice, every cranny of these mountains.

There was no place to hide from him.

Suddenly he smelled Linara more sharply than before.

She wasn't running away from him, but toward him. She grew closer; he heard her breath come hard and when he listened to it, he heard her heart pounding. She was in a hurry. Why was she rushing up the mountain?

He was about to find out.

She ran around the corner, saw him, and stopped. He flapped his wings once, beginning his ascent. It was a natural reaction, to move away from her sword, to place himself into an optimal position to rain fire upon her. With a sudden and powerful burst, Linara ran toward him, shouting. Screaming, "No!"

He no longer wondered why she'd come back. His stolen sword was raised against him as she rushed directly into his path, as she ran beneath his left wing and swung wildly.

The agony was intense, the weakness immediate. How had she known he was vulnerable there? No one knew. No one could know. Once the dragon hunters had discovered their weakness, it had signaled the end of his kind. How had she found...?

Ah, yes. Demon.

A sharp pain seared through him as he dropped down so hard the mountain shuddered, as what felt like his own fire whipped down his side, through his entire body. The dragon could not fly, not like this. He looked at Linara, prepared to breathe fire upon her, and then he saw her face. Through a dragon's eyes, she was sharply in focus, the colors of the rainbow in and around her, the tears in her eyes and on her face sparkling like diamonds. He held the flame and turned away from her. Was this a demon's trick? A woman's trick?

Her words reached him through a fog of pain. "Do not fly. Do not breathe fire into the night sky. He thinks you're dead." Linara dropped his sword and reached out her hands to touch his wing, to caress near to where she'd cut him. "I'm sorry. So sorry, but..."

He turned his head and she looked directly, without fear or hate, into his eye.

"I can't let him kill you. He sent me; he sent the Caradon. He will send someone else if he thinks I failed."

Pax dropped down, resting his wounded wing on the ground, laying his head on the stony path. Any sane woman would run. Linara had accomplished what she'd set out to do. He was grounded until his wing could heal. He was not dead, but he was worthless. She could finish him in short order, and with his own sword. The sword she'd discarded.

Instead of running away, as any right-thinking human would have, Linara sat beside him, leaning into him. Her hands caressed his neck. "You are so beautiful," she whispered. "As a man, as a dragon...you are magnificent. It would be beyond evil to remove you from this world." She kissed him, placed her soft lips against his scaly neck. He had not thought he'd ever feel such a gentle touch there, but he did. "Let me protect you. Let me keep you safe."

Pax closed his eyes. He would heal quicker in his natural form. He wasn't sure how bad the wound would be if he shifted into his human body now. Linara rested against him. She had wounded him, and for that he should cook her. But she had apparently done so in a foolish attempt to save him.

When he was human again, they would talk. There had been far too much unsaid between them.

The sky began to lighten, a dull gray that signaled morning was coming. Linara held on, and soon she slept. Eventually, so did he.

Linara dreamed of killing Naal, and woke shivering even though the sun was high in the sky and the air was mild, almost warm. Still, she shivered.

The pack of Caradon had been sent to kill Pax. Naal would have murdered her without regret. He'd deserved nothing but death, and yet she did regret taking his life. In spite of who she was, despite the demon blood within her, she had never before killed anyone or anything. Was her aura darker now? Was she unredeemable?

She curled into a ball against Pax's neck. When she had seen him spread his wings to rise she'd acted on instinct, bringing him down. It would not do for anyone to see the dragon in the night sky. If Stasio realized that the images she had shared with him were false, not only would he send someone — or something — else for Pax, Sophie Fyne Varden and everyone else Linara loved would be in danger.

Yes, loved. The circumstances of her conception and birth should have made it impossible for her, but she did love. Her mother, her father, her entire family. She loved and was loved. She had been surrounded by love all her life. There had been times when her jealousy had overwhelmed that love, but she could no longer deny the power of it.

Pax, the dragon and the man, she loved him, too.

She would never tell. What man or beast could love what she was? Maybe one day, if the witch Lyssa could truly remove the darkness of the demon from her as she had done for others, love might be possible for her. Maybe one day, if she could be certain the poison within her was gone, a man might wish to claim her as his own. She wanted to be cherished, the way Kane Varden cherished Sophie Fyne. She wanted a love for the ages.

Was such a miracle even possible for her? Was being the first, the most powerful, the one for whom an entire class of demon was named...could that be stripped away?

Most powerful. Ha. She did not feel powerful, she never had.

Pax opened his eyes. Well, he opened the one she could see from her vantage point, at least. She could not be sure about the other. It was a beautiful eye, dark like those of the man she knew, but also alive with red and orange and yellow, as if his fire somehow lived there.

She stroked his neck with one hand. Heavens, she liked the feel of him. Man or dragon, she could not get enough of touching him. The colors of his scales were much like the mountain pond where they had made love. Blue and green, sparkling in a way nothing else could. "If I knew with any certainty that you understood, I would leave now. I have a job to do. Kill Stasio. Make sure my family is safe. Perhaps find the witch who might..." Fix her? Cure her? She wasn't sure. "Then, if you will have me, I can return. You asked me to stay with you, once. Knowing what you know now, would you ask again?"

She could read no answer in his eye.

"I will die if he kills you."

It was the truth, a hard admission to make.

Could she leave him here? Could she protect him at all costs? If the prophecies were correct, if Stasio had been right, Pax was necessary for the end of the war, for the defeat of the daughters of the Isen Demon like her.

"I have much to tell you when you are a man again, and I'm certain you understand." Maybe he could understand her now. Maybe not. "Heal, Pax. Heal, and then we will decide what to do. Together."

The rain promised by last night's clouds began to fall. Pax's wounded wing fluttered up and down again, sheltering her from the cold, gentle drops. Raindrops rolled off his wing and dropped to the ground, but she remained dry.

She still did not know with certainty how he felt about her, but his protection from the elements was a good sign.

CHAPTER 14

"Rain's coming," Cyrus said.

As they had yesterday, the trio rode in a column. They continued to the north, because Val instinctively knew that was where she was needed. The general led the way. Of course he did. Val rode in the middle, determined to keep her companions — one demon, one a man she cared for — apart. For the safety of the one who was not a shapeshifting demon, of course. She hadn't slept a wink last night, so she kept yawning and closing her eyes in unnecessarily long blinks. It wasn't very warrior-like. Her mind was spinning, but her body was exhausted.

"I'm not afraid of getting wet," General Merin — or not General Merin — said without bothering to look back.

"We'll need to rest the horses soon in any case," Val said. "Keep an eye out for a place we might stay dry."

Could she sleep tonight? Did she dare?

Cyrus agreed. Val's father grudgingly did the same. It was her father who spotted the dilapidated barn in the distance. They all turned in that direction.

She had searched for clues in the men who accompanied her, and found none. It was annoying. Uryen had apparently learned from her initial mistakes with Cyrus.

A couple of times during the day Val had planned how she might simply slip away. As the others slept. When she went to a pond or a stream to wash up. Maybe when she excused herself for personal matters. She was meant to make this journey on her own! But no. If she left, whichever one was Uryen in disguise might well decide to dispose of the other. The demon was afraid of Val. She was not afraid of anything or anyone else.

And so Val remained.

What she needed was a test of some sort. A way to force Uryen to reveal her true self. She had not yet thought of a proper test, and so they rode on.

A light rain began to fall not long before they reached the barn. The cool mist felt good on Val's skin. It was invigorating, at a time when she could use it. Neither of the men with her seemed to be bothered at all by the rain.

They were settled under cover, the horses fed and lightly brushed, before the storm was upon them. The barn leaked here and there, but they were all able to claim a dry spot. Maybe they could sleep, and if the rain stopped before sunrise they could set out earlier than usual.

There was no fire tonight, but Cyrus found an old oil lamp and lit it, so they were not in complete darkness.

After they'd passed around water and nuts and oatcakes, her father closed his eyes and seemed to go to sleep instantly. It was an annoying habit he had, being able to sleep anywhere and everywhere. He did not toss and turn. Ever. Was that a sign he was who he claimed to be? Not really.

Cyrus was more prone to fidgeting. He did toss and turn. Constantly.

Since leaving Forbidden Mountain, Val normally fell asleep with her mind spinning, trusting that Kitty would wake her if necessary. Since she hadn't slept last night, it was unlikely she could stay awake tonight even if she wanted to. Was it safe to sleep? It certainly wasn't safe for her to continue without it.

Sleep came quickly, as she listened to the patter of rain on what remained of the barn roof. The dreams came soon after. She dreamed, as she so often did, of dragons and death. Of war and treachery. Normally in her dreams she had an army behind her, but on this night they had all turned against her. She was the enemy. She trusted no one and they did not trust her.

Kitty hummed, and Val woke with a start to see Cyrus at her side, so close she was instantly alarmed. He had a hand on Kitty's blade. No, that was just one finger. One long, sun-browned finger where it did not belong. She did not know how much time had passed since she'd fallen asleep, but the lamp still burned. The rain had moved on, and bright moonlight shone through the wide spaces in the roof. She could see her friend...or not her friend...clearly.

"What are you doing?" she snapped, sitting up and snatching Kitty from him. Him or her? Uryen again, trying to take Kitty while Val slept? Val leaped to her feet and took a fighting stance.

Cyrus rose to his feet, too, though not as smoothly as she had. "I...I was just...I couldn't sleep, and I swear it seemed the sword was whispering to me..."

Heavens above, it was her. Uryen wore Cyrus' face again. This time she would have to kill the demon. She had no choice. Her grip tightened. She prepared every muscle in her body for what had to be done.

Her mind was not ready. She hesitated.

"Do it," her father whispered. "Kill him. He betrayed you. You are destined to kill him. *Her*," he corrected. "Kill *her*."

Val did not relax her stance, but she did close her eyes. Gods, that was not her father. Not entirely his voice. Not his words at all.

Could she take the head of a demon who wore her father's face?

What choice did she have?

"What are you waiting for?" Uryen whispered.

Val spun around on one heel. Kitty rose, smooth and deadly. Tears clouding her vision, Val leaped toward her father. Not her father, really, but that was her father's face, his eyes, his stance. If she hesitated, if she allowed herself to think, all would be lost. She had no time for second thoughts, for wondering if she was right or not. This could not be a mistake.

No, that voice, those words…

It had to be quick. No hesitation. No second thoughts. And still, she did not see a demon before her. She saw the man who had raised her. Father, teacher, a husband who loved his wife. No one, not even his children, could make Tearlach Merin smile the way Bela did. He had taught Val to wield a sword, to fight with her hands, to survive when others might not. He'd laughed at her, hugged her, told her he was proud of her.

And that was his face.

Val swung her sword with strength, with determination. The tears in her eyes made the face she loved go blurry, and that was a gift.

Just before the blade met flesh, those eyes flashed red and her father — Uryen — screeched.

Val screamed, as what appeared to be her father's head was separated from his body. While that head was in midair, it changed. The hair turned to flame for a moment. The body shifted to that of a slender woman as it dropped to the ground.

And Val continued to scream.

The horses, alarmed by the shrill sounds, whinnied and danced, but thank goodness they were well tethered and could not escape.

Val looked at what remained of Uryen, but in her mind, she still saw her father standing there as she took his head. She saw his face, his curly hair with just a few grays she had given him over the years, and she screamed again.

Eventually, she realized that Cyrus' hands were on her shoulders, and he spoke to her.

"It's over."

No, it has barely begun.

"That was not your father. I should have known."

I should have known.

"It's going to be all right."

At that, Val jerked away and spun on Cyrus. "All right? Have you lost your mind? Nothing is all right. I just killed my father."

"You killed the demon you were destined to kill." His voice was maddeningly calm.

"But she looked like my father. When I took her head…" She saw it again, and again, in her mind. Her knees went out from under her, and she dropped to them because she no longer had the strength to stand. The tears came, harsh and ugly, and again she screamed.

Cyrus dropped, too. He wrapped his arms around her. She jerked away, but when he grabbed her again, she fell into him and cried even harder.

"I hate this! I hate it all!"

It was Kitty who whispered, *This is who you are,*

Valora. It is who I am.

"Don't cry," Cyrus whispered as he held her close. He even ran one hand through her unruly hair.

Cry, Kitty said forcefully. *Cry while you can. It is a luxury you will not have for much longer.*

The rain stopped, and Linara left the shelter of Pax's wing. By the light of the morning sun, she studied the wound that had brought him down. The wound — delivered by her hand wielding his sword — seemed to have healed a bit. Not enough to suit her. How quickly did a dragon heal? How could she possibly know?

She wondered if it was possible that healing was one of her gifts. You wouldn't think a demon might possess such a power, but anything was possible. Aunt Juliet was a talented healer, and though Linara had no Fyne blood in her veins, the influence existed. It thrived. That influence was what had kept her from being the terror she'd been born to be.

She had never realized how strong that influence had been, until she'd tried to deny it.

Pax's eyes opened. He turned his large head slowly and looked at her. She saw it all in his eyes. Pain. Anger. Betrayal. He could decide to kill her here and now. Or later. Or tomorrow. Was one ever truly safe with a dragon? Especially a betrayed dragon.

She would not run. She would not leave him. If he ended her life, then so be it.

"I would like to look at your wound. Can you lift your wing a bit so I can see?"

One eye narrowed. At that moment she could see the similarity between the man and the dragon. The slant. The arch. The sarcasm.

"Yes, I realize I'm the one who cut you. You know why, so don't give me that look." He did understand, didn't he? Otherwise, she'd already be dead.

The wounded wing lifted slightly, and Linara peeked beneath to study the injury more closely. She winced at the ugliness of it, at the gash so near to where she'd slept while it rained. There was little blood. She didn't know if that was because of the location or if dragons simply didn't bleed much.

There was so much she didn't know.

She lifted her hand to the edge of the gash nearest Pax's body. *Heal.* She thought the word, and then she whispered it. In the shadow of his wing, she could easily make out the colors that emanated from her fingers. Those tendrils of color touched him, they whipped around and then inside the tear in his flesh. He flinched.

That flinch knocked her back so hard she flew out from the shadows. She lost her breath for a moment. From her new position on her backside, she could see the dragon's face well.

He looked far too pleased with himself.

"I'm trying to help you," she snapped.

His expression told her nothing.

For years, Stasio had spoken to her. She had, on more than one occasion, shared thoughts with her half-demon sisters. Could she touch the dragon's mind as she had on the night they'd first met?

She sat up straight and — before proceeding — made sure the wall she had built against Stasio was strong. He could not see this, could not know the dragon lived. That done, she rocked onto her knees and leaned toward Pax's large and beautiful head. The scales there possessed all the colors of the rainbow, in darker hues. His wings were beautiful shades of green and blue, but his face possessed more color.

"I'm going to touch you now," she warned. "Don't knock me back, please."

One eye narrowed, and again, she saw the man in the beast.

Moving slowly, she reached toward him. Her fingers brushed against his face. He did not throw her off. Her palm pressed against his scales, and when the touch felt right, she closed her eyes and reached for him.

Yes, he was there. Yes, she could touch his mind. She almost jerked away; she did flinch. But she made herself stay. She did not break the physical connection.

The language of the dragon was one she did not know, and could not speak even if she did understand. The words in Pax's mind were guttural and harsh, grinding and sharp. Before she could ask him to shift his thoughts to those she could understand, he felt her confusion and did so on his own.

You cut me.

I told you why.

I am not afraid of your wizard. Was it he who told you I was vulnerable beneath my wing?

No one told me. I just swung wildly. Call it luck.

Bad luck, for me. You do the work of your wizard. Do not deny it.

He will kill my mother if he discovers that I did not complete my task.

There was silence for a long moment as Pax took in that information.

Your mother...

The woman who raised me after my birth mother died. Sophie Fyne Varden. You would like her.

She felt his puzzlement, not in words but as an emotion. *I like no one.*

Linara smiled. *You like me.*

Grudging acceptance.

I brought you down not only to save you, but to save her. Stasio must believe you are dead.

I am not afraid...

He is afraid of you. Otherwise, he would not have been so desperate to see you dead.

I will kill him. That thought was expressed with

such fierce emotion, Linara allowed her hand to fall.

And still, she heard Pax's thoughts. They remained connected. *But first I must heal. Do what you must. I will not throw you off again.*

Sitting beside him, legs crossed, sunlight on her face, Linara pressed her fingers against his scales and then, with ease, slid into her healing mode. She knew the ministrations hurt, maybe as much as the wound itself had. *Forgive me?*

There was a bit more of that guttural language, followed by thoughts she could understand well.

Not yet.

CHAPTER 15

Warriors should not cry. They should certainly not sob off and on for days.

Val swiped a sleeve across her cheek. She knew the being she had beheaded had not been her father. She knew it had been Uryen wearing her father's face. And still the image stayed with her. In her too-frequent remembering she never saw the demon after death, no, she always saw her father before and while the blade cut into his neck and ended his life.

Maybe she was a warrior, but still...her first kill had been a demon who wore the face of her father. She would never forget it, never erase that horrible memory from her mind.

Kitty had been unrelentingly pragmatic. *Stop crying. Cease. You did what had to be done, you have fulfilled the first part of your prophecy.* And when those words did not make any difference, the magical sword had gone silent. Val had not known a sword could grumble and then give the silent treatment, but that's what Kitty did.

Cyrus understood. He didn't tell her not to cry. When she found a private place in the evening to simply let go and sob, he took care of the horses and built a fire without a word of complaint. He caught meat for their dinner and cooked it. Now and then he asked her if she wanted to talk. She never did.

She wouldn't allow him to physically coddle her as he had immediately after the incident, even though there were times when she wanted very much to be coddled.

The more disturbing episodes, those where she wept until her eyes were burning and swollen and her chest hurt and she occasionally gave a scream of frustration, ceased after a couple of days. Tears occasionally dribbled down her face, and she got the hiccups far too frequently, and the vision of her father — *not* her father — remained. Reality helped her to heal. She began to focus on the memory of Uryen's body on ground, Uryen's flaming hair, Uryen's screech.

She had done what needed to be done. It had been painful, but she'd survived. Cyrus had survived.

Her father had survived.

The barn was five days behind them when they stopped to camp by a small, clear pond. The foothills were only a day or two away. From there, onward and upward. And upward. She felt as if she were being drawn there, as if she had no choice in the matter at all.

Clear-eyed and hiccup-free, Val sat beside the fire Cyrus had built and put on her fiercest face. "Tomorrow morning, you will return to the village."

Surprisingly, Cyrus was as determined as she.

"No."

Val sighed. "You are no soldier, and before much longer I will be in the middle of a war." She could feel it coming. Close, so close.

"I am aware."

"How can you be so unconcerned about your life? I'm trying to protect you!"

He was much calmer than she as he responded, "As I am trying to protect you."

Seriously? "I don't need protection."

Kitty, who had been silent for days, finally spoke. *Let him tag along.* Why now? It wasn't as if Kitty had expressed any fondness for Cyrus before now.

"You are destined to go to war, but no prophecy ever said you would fight alone," Cyrus said. "You are to lead an army. I want to be a part of that army."

"You're a farmer!" It was meant to be an insult, but judging by his expression, it was not taken as such. How else was she supposed to scare him away?

He remained calm, as usual. "Very few warriors are trained from birth, as you were. Soldiers are also blacksmiths and bakers, shepherds and yes, even farmers."

"You are no..." She'd intended to say warrior, but something in Cyrus' eyes stopped her. He was determined. He was dedicated. At that moment he looked every bit the warrior.

"Fine," she snapped. "But you are free to go at any time."

"I have always been free to go at any time," he said in an even voice.

It was true.

Kitty vibrated with some excitement, and she all but shouted, for Val's ears alone, *They're coming! Get ready!*

At that moment she heard someone — several someones — drawing near. Horses, at least a dozen. Gods! She had been so lost in her conversation, she'd let her guard down.

She caught Cyrus' eye. "You want to be a soldier? I think your chance has arrived."

At that moment, he heard, too. He did not have a sword, but he wore two knives on his belt, and he pulled them both.

More than a dozen, Val judged as the riders came closer. Perhaps double that number. Should they run? The odds were not in their favor. They could not know that those who approached meant them harm, but...

We do not retreat, Kitty said with some disdain.

Kitty in hand, Val stood on a boulder to the north side of their camp and waited. She could see them now, shadows in the night. Twenty riders. Her heart climbed into her throat. Twenty against two, and Cyrus...

She dismissed that concern. Cyrus was a fighter, too. She could see it in his stance as he stood on the ground beside her, knives at the ready.

Knives which would not do him any good at all

if the riders came in with swords swinging.

They did not approach like attackers, which caused her to relax a bit. Just a bit. Still, they moved forward with purpose; they weren't a group of hunters out to provide for their families on this fine evening. No, they were soldiers.

Finally, the leader of the riders came into view, and for the first time in her entire life, Val dropped her sword. Kitty protested as she bounced off stone and then hit the ground, but Val paid her no mind. She jumped off the boulder and ran. The tears she had worked so hard to shed came roaring back. Her heart pounded.

Her father leaped off his horse and caught her as she threw herself at him. She held on tight, and so did he. She sobbed again; her tears dampened his shoulder. That was his smell, his heartbeat, his warmth. How had she ever been fooled?

"What's wrong?" he snapped.

"Nothing," Val managed to say between sobs.

"Something is wrong."

Her father ordered the men to restrain Cyrus, after judging that he was likely the reason for Val's reaction. That ended Val's tears. She lifted her head and jumped down and back, wiping away tears with one hand.

She turned to order the men not to lay a finger on her friend, but that order was unnecessary.

Kitty hovered in the air, dancing before Cyrus, threatening any who came close. Her blade was quick and sharp, and the wise soldiers steered clear.

"That's my friend, Cyrus. He is not the reason I cried." She turned around and faced her father again, and this time she smiled as she reached up to lay her palms on his cheeks. "Have I ever told you that I love your face?"

A dragon should heal faster!

Her attempts were not entirely wasted, but the results were far too slow. She wanted to wave her hand and have it done, but they'd been here for days and the healing was not complete.

Without warning, the dragon moved. He shifted his weight in a way he had not in the days since she'd cut him.

"You cannot fly," she reminded him, not for the first time. It was dark. If the dragon breathed fire, someone would see. Stasio might find out.

I can, Pax directed her way. He looked at her. *But I won't. Not yet.*

He took a wobbly stance, head down, wings dropped. He stood that way for a moment, and then he slowly and deliberately lifted his head. Pax looked to the sky as if he craved it. Maybe he did, but he understood the risk.

Did he care that showing himself would put her mother in danger? Of course not. Why would he?

His wings came up, stronger than they had been in days, as beautiful as they had been the first time she saw them. She waited for him to take flight, to undo everything she had tried to do...

But that wasn't what happened.

She watched as he changed, shrinking in on himself. Flesh replaced scales. Hair replaced the horns on his head. Pax was in pain as he shifted; she felt that pain as if it were her own. The damage she had done to the underside of his wing remained, an oozing cut down his side and on the inside of his arm from armpit to elbow.

If he had shifted immediately after she'd cut him, the man would not have survived. What would have happened to the dragon in that case?

She did not want to know.

He walked to her, taking long strides on the hard ground. Those eyes — Pax's eyes; dragon's eyes — she should have known all along...

And then he stood before her, naked, wounded, and angry. Angry with her, with the wizard in the lands below, and with himself.

She had apologized to the dragon, and now she did the same to the man. "I'm so sorry. I could think of no other way..."

With his uninjured arm, he grabbed her. He placed his hand on the back of her head and pulled her close. The kiss was brutal, harsh, and beautiful. It fed her, as nothing and no one else could. He forgave her. He must. If not, how could he kiss her this way? How could he give so much of himself to her, if not for...love? She had never believed love was for her. She was death; she was demon. Who could love a demon whose very touch was death?

Pax. Pax loved her.

She touched him as they kissed, running her fingers over his skin from waist to armpit and then down again. She brushed his arm; she held him close.

And when he ended the kiss, he was wounded no more.

He rested his forehead on hers. "You were growing weak," he whispered. "I felt it. You needed to be fed, and no one feeds you as the dragon does."

Linara's spirits fell. Her heart dropped to the cold stone ground they stood upon. Pax didn't love her. He needed her. He'd needed her to be powerful enough to heal him, so he could...

Leave her? Kill her? Either would be painful.

"My need had not reached a critical stage." Though...he was right. She had begun to hunger.

She felt his anger as if it were a tangible thing, a wave in the ocean or a stiff breeze that whipped the trees. And yet there was something more than anger. He wanted her, still. He hated and desired her, craved and despised her.

She loved him, no matter how he felt about her. They were connected now in a way they had not been before. Did he feel her love, or was it washed away by his fury? She did her best to hide what she felt. Deception was a gift she possessed that he did not.

Linara took a step away and pulled her shift over her head, so she was as naked as he. "A kiss is not the only way you can feed me," she said without emotion. "If you are of a mind, of course." She knew he was; he was aroused, and had been from the moment he'd shifted.

She reached for him, craving his body, wanting his love and knowing she would never have it.

And determined not to allow him to see the impossible love within her.

CHAPTER 16

There had been a time when Pax had been gentle with this woman, when he'd laid her upon fur skins and touched her with some tenderness. Tonight he showed her none. He was not gentle. Linara was a demon, not a fragile woman. She did not need or deserve tenderness.

It was not as though it was in his nature to care.

She fed on him, and he gladly gave her what she needed. He fed on her, too, in a way he had never expected.

He fucked her on the rocky ground, with no fur rug, with no pretense. This was the only dance they would ever know, a meeting of bodies in need, a joining in search of physical pleasure and blessed release.

Linara was nothing more to him, no matter what she said, no matter that she insisted she'd been trying to protect him when she'd brought him down. She'd wounded him to save her mother, who was probably a demon as dark and heartless as she.

Tonight as she found release she parted her lips to scream as she had the last time he'd lain with her. That sound had called the Caradon upon them. He clamped his mouth to hers and smothered her scream. He pressed her into the ground as she convulsed around him, and then he found his release.

He did not scream; he did not make a sound, other than a low growl which would alarm no one.

For a moment, Linara looked vulnerable. Her expression softened; her eyes widened. Then she hardened those eyes and placed a steady hand on his cheek. "Come with me to the valley," she whispered.

"Why?"

"You said you wanted to kill Stasio."

"I don't need you to do that."

He rolled away from her, still feeling her around him, still smelling her on his skin. He needed to bathe, but there was no pond nearby. A good hard rainstorm would do, he supposed, but the skies were clear.

As he looked up, clouds rolled in. Moments later, a hard rain fell, soaking him and Linara. He looked at her accusingly and shouted to be heard above the hard rain.

"Get out of my head!"

The rain stopped as suddenly as it had started.

Linara sat a few feet away, naked and soaking wet, vulnerable and powerful.

"I killed a man," she said, her voice so low a human might've missed the meaning. "He was one of the Caradon who attacked us, and he…he had ill intentions."

She did not describe these ill intentions, but he could imagine. He should not feel anger toward the shifter, but he did. He pushed that reaction down, rejected it. "Then he deserved to die."

"Perhaps he did, but I still felt a stain on my soul as I fed on him." She shook her wet head, and at last her voice rose to a normal level. "I can't embrace the darkness and survive. I...I can't."

Pax growled. "You want me to accompany you off this mountain and into the valley because you need me to feed you." First anger, now disappointment. He needed to get away from this woman as soon as possible.

"Yes. I need you until I reach my mother and she can provide another amulet that will end my demon hunger."

"An amulet," he repeated.

"Yes. I had one, but I...I threw it away. I thought it had become a crutch, but it was not. It was a precious gift."

She could do anything. Heal. Hurt. Bring rain when there should be none. And then end that rain in a heartbeat. Why couldn't she...

"I tried to make a replacement. For days, I tried. I can't. I don't have the right magic."

"Get out of my head," he said again.

"I would if I could," she snapped. She jumped to her feet, all pale skin and wet hair and gentle strength.

She had great breasts...

He turned his thoughts to other things.

"There might be another way, a witch…" She stopped speaking, pursed her lips. "But I don't even know if that will work, or where this witch is, or…but none of that matters. You are here now. You are the only way." Her expression changed, as she left behind all doubts, all softness. "You will need clothes," she snapped. "The trousers and shirt of the Caradon I killed are south of here. They're a bit dusty, and I don't think they'll fit well, but I suppose they'll do until we can find you something more appropriate."

"I won't wear any stinking Caradon…"

"Fine," she snapped. "Wear this." She threw her soaking wet white shift to him. It landed in his lap with a cool slap of the thin fabric.

Pax peeled the shift away and tossed it aside.

Maybe the clothes of a stinking Caradon wouldn't be so bad after all.

Cyrus sat away from the fire, not because he didn't want its warmth, but because the closer he got to Val, the harder General Merin glared at him.

The fake General Merin, the one Val had beheaded, had on occasion tossed what Cyrus now knew to be an obligatory fatherly stare his way. If he had ever before been on the receiving end of this, he would have known in an instant that the man they'd met on the trail was an impostor.

The stare of a demon had not made Cyrus cringe the way this one did.

It was natural, he supposed, for a father to be protective of his daughter. How could he assure the general that he had no ill intentions toward Val? He only wanted to help her. That's all he had ever wanted.

Well, for now.

Cyrus had spent most of his life dreaming of things to come. The leather scabbard he'd fashioned for Kitty was only one of those things. The dreams didn't come every night. They didn't even come every year. But they did come.

He'd never spoken of the prophetic dreams to his family. His mother was distrustful of magic of any kind, and he didn't want to upset her needlessly. His father wasn't afraid of witches and wizards, but he was a down-to-earth man who worked the land and cared for nothing else but that land and his family.

So Cyrus kept his dreams to himself. He had acted on occasion, in a surreptitious manner. He'd faked an illness once to keep his mother away from the market where she would have fallen and hurt her hip. That fall would've left her with a limp, and constant pain, for the rest of her life. He'd tossed out the roasted meat that would have made the entire family sick. His mother had been furious, but he'd taken his punishment and kept the secret she did not want to know.

There had been no momentous dreams. He was not meant to save the world as Val was.

He liked her. She was prettier than a warrior should be, as well as younger. She fussed about her hair now and then, but he liked it. Her hair was dark and wild and curly, and there was a lot of it.

A few years after the war was done, if they both survived, he was going to marry her.

No wonder General Merin glared.

Cyrus slept, but he did not sleep well. He dreamed.

The sun rose. To the north, the mountains seemed closer than ever before. In a few days, they'd be there. Soon, Val's part in it all would begin.

Val was readying her horse when General Merin approached Cyrus with his scowl in place. "You should go home, boy. No matter what my daughter says, you're not a soldier."

Like daughter, like father.

It would be easy to nod and go. Back to the farm, back to his family.

"My apologies, sir, but I can't do that."

His hands curled into fists. "Why not?"

"Val needs me."

"I'm here now."

"You need me, too. Sir," he added belatedly.

"I assure you…"

Cyrus pointed toward the mountains. "Before you reach the foothills, you will be attacked by an army of demons. Women your men will hesitate to kill, because to their eyes they will initially appear to be ordinary females, like their wives and daughters. I assure you, they are anything but ordinary."

The general's jaw clenched, and then he asked, with rancor, "How can you possibly know this?"

All his life, Cyrus had hidden his ability. He had not even told Val everything. Perhaps it was time he trusted someone. "I dreamed of it last night."

"A dream…"

"As I dreamed of Kitty's scabbard. As I dreamed of a danger to my mother I was able to avert." He fisted his hands in frustration. No, he would not tell General Merin that he had dreamed of a fully grown Valora Merin as his wife. There was more than one way to die in this war. "As I have dreamed of events to come all my life."

Val's father narrowed his eyes, more suspicious than angry. "If you are some wizard, why didn't your dreams tell you that Uryen was impersonating me?"

Cyrus felt a blush heat his cheeks. Wizard? No, it couldn't be that. It would be too much to grasp. He just had a gift, that's all. He did not want to be a wizard, did not wish ever to be a seer people sought out for answers to fix their lives. It would be too much responsibility, a burden. Gods, he did not want to show his emotions to the general! He forced himself to take a long, deep breath before explaining. "The dreams come to me. I do not choose. I never have."

General Merin was a man accustomed to the ways of magic. He would know and accept that there were no rules.

After a too long and somewhat uncomfortable silence, General Merin nodded once and said, "You can remain with us, if you choose."

Cyrus choked on the words, "Thank you, sir." He was glad of the acceptance, no matter how unwilling it might be. No matter what Val's father said, he wasn't going anywhere.

Naturally, Naal's clothes did not fit Pax well. Linara looked him up and down. Naal had not been a thin man, but he'd not been near Pax's size. The pants had split, here and there, and the shirt fit no better.

"We'll find you more suitable clothing further down this path," she said.

Pax snorted. "Are you going to suck the life out of a larger man, or is there a market I know nothing about in a cave around the next corner?"

There was no need for him to be so harsh. His voice was caustic. Angry. He had not forgiven her for cutting him with the sword he carried. A weapon he kept close, now.

"I don't want to kill again," she said.

"But that doesn't mean you won't."

Her anger rushed to the surface. "This is war. How many have you killed?"

His face was stony; his eyes went darker than usual. "I have done my best to avoid your war. A mere handful of invaders have tasted my fire."

If Pax had enjoyed killing, if he had been a man of war, he would have left this mountain long ago and thrown himself into battle.

He had hidden here much as she had hidden in Stasio's shadow. The time had come for both of them to choose. To fight.

"We're only a day or two from the foothills," she said in a calmer voice. "There are isolated farms not far south. We will make do."

"I have stolen clothing before," he said. "Sometimes it is necessary."

She could imagine. The dragon could fly long distances in a short period, and she had not seen the beast with any pack on its back or tied to a leg. She could not even imagine how he might make that work. Of course, he had stolen clothing!

"After I am clothed to your satisfaction, what's the plan?"

"We're going to travel to the village where I once lived, and we'll kill Stasio." She didn't mention the witch who might strip away the demonic part of herself. Why? She didn't know if Lyssa was alive, if she was anywhere near, or if she would do what Linara desired. Could she be just a woman? It was almost too much to hope for. She could not let herself even imagine.

At the mention of Stasio, Pax turned his anger

from her. She could almost see his emotions shift. "I'll end that one myself. Even the toughest of wizards can burn."

"He will see you coming. He will be prepared."

Pax stared at her. "So will I."

CHAPTER 17

Pax wanted to shift into dragon form, fly to the village Linara spoke of, and burn them all. He would do just that, but he was not yet at full strength, and he would not be facing just one man. If the demons there knew he was coming — and they would if he approached from a distance — they would be ready to take him down with their dark magic and their swords. He'd seen many of his kind brought down with that combination. Before he flew into the village, he needed to be at full strength, and he needed a plan.

He had never been one for planning. The dragon flew. As man and as beast, he ate. He slept. His life had always been simple. He took what he wanted when he wanted it. He bowed to no man. Or woman.

There had been a time when he would have gladly bowed to her.

Before she'd died, his mother had promised him that one day he would have a proper mate. He'd searched the world over, hoping to find another of his kind, determined not to be the last dragon. It was possible to sleep for a long time, in his natural state. Perhaps a female, the one meant for him, slept the years away, thinking there was no hope, no mate for her.

With every day that passed, the hope within him died. There was no mate for him. Maybe it was time for him to fly blindly into battle and die a warrior's death. He had nothing left to live for.

If he survived this war and his prophesied part in it, he would return to mountains far from these, where he had spent most of his life. They were grand mountains where no human had lived for hundreds of years. Years ago, the dragons had fought back, and the humans who had survived that war had moved on. As he had. He'd return there, he would settle in a cave that sparkled with dragonstone, and he would sleep for a thousand years.

And when he woke, the world would be changed. Perhaps there would be a place for him in it.

There was no place for him in this one.

Val had been so sure her father was going to force Cyrus to go home! But he had not. Since their early morning conversation just two days ago, a conversation Val had watched with an interest she'd tried to disguise, something had changed. She just couldn't be sure what.

Her father no longer looked at Cyrus as if he were willing his head to explode. She guessed that was an improvement of sorts. Cyrus did continue to keep his distance from the rest of the traveling party.

He did not speak to her father or her father's soldiers. He rarely spoke to her.

It wouldn't be long before the sun set, and they made camp for the night. A part of her wanted to keep riding, to forgo sleep and push toward their destination. Only for the horses could she be convinced to rest through the night.

She didn't think she'd have a chance to talk to Cyrus later in the evening; her father was weirdly protective of her when they were in camp. So she edged Snowflake to the side, then slowed a bit and gradually moved closer to Cyrus and his sturdy mount.

"You've been quiet lately," she said in a casual tone.

Cyrus scoffed, a bit. "Your father doesn't like it when I speak."

"Oh, don't be…" She stopped before saying, "silly," because her father turned his head and glared in her direction. "He means well," she said.

"I would never hurt you," Cyrus said. He sounded so serious!

"Of course you wouldn't. I'm difficult to injure, in any case."

Cyrus turned her head and glared, much as her father had. "There are ways to be hurt that have nothing to do with weapons and war."

Kitty hummed. *He likes you.*

Of course he liked her. They were friends. Val's insides thumped and fluttered. That's not the kind of liking Kitty was talking about. Cyrus was a couple of years older than she was, and handsome enough to have any girl he wanted. Kitty was teasing. Or else just wrong in her assumptions.

I don't tease, and I'm never wrong.

Val lifted her chin and looked at Cyrus, who continued to keep his gaze trained ahead. She tried to think of something appropriate to say to him. Anything that wouldn't embarrass her, or reveal that she liked him, too, more than she should. Perhaps the day would come…

Cyrus pulled his horse to a stop and raised one hand. "That stand of trees, do you see?"

Val looked where he was pointing. It was an ordinary clump of ordinary trees, if you discounted the enormous gnarled, dead tree to the west. Everything else was appropriately green. "Well, yes. What about it?"

Cyrus spurred his horse forward, and Val followed. What was he doing? He seemed to be heading straight to her father. This could *not* be good.

"Sir," Cyrus snapped when he reached the general. "That's it, that's the place I told you about."

"You're sure," her father said, squinting toward the grove.

"Positive."

"They're watching."

"I would assume so, sir," Cyrus replied.

Val remained silent as her father raised his voice slightly to speak to his men. "We're about to be ambushed," he said. "In that grove ahead, there waits a small army of women who are not all they appear to be. They are demons. They will kill us all if we allow it to happen."

A soldier close by muttered. "I knew we would face women in battle, but as the time grows close...I have my reservations."

It was Val who said, "Then you will die, and after you die those demons will turn their darkness upon your wives and sisters and daughters. Kill them now, or allow them to win. If they win, they will destroy all that you love."

That soldier, and others in their party, seemed to set aside their doubts. They could not allow a child to be braver and more determined than they.

Kitty sang, anxious for battle.

"Do we have a plan?" Val asked.

Her father smiled. "We do."

Linara looked over the valley. She and Pax had made good time. There was more green here. The wooded foothills were not far below.

Since leaving home, since running away in the night, she had been searching for a purpose. At first, she'd thought to leave her home and family behind and become what she'd been born to be. Demon. She would never be like them, good and kind and *normal.* Well, as normal as a witch and her brood could be.

It had not taken her long to discover that no matter the circumstances of her birth, she was not like the other daughters of the Isen Demon. At least, she was not like the others Stasio had called to him. They delighted in killing; they embraced all their dark powers. She had not.

Then a purpose had been given to her. Kill the dragon. She had failed that mission, as well.

Now she had a new purpose, one she embraced. Stasio had to die. Without him, would the demon army fall? Would it at least be weakened? Could she finally accomplish the task she'd set out to do?

No other mission had ever felt this important.

And after that? She had no idea what would happen then. She wasn't human, nor was she entirely demon. She could never know love, not as a human might. Her touch was poison to any man. She glanced to the side, to a silent, brooding Pax. Except for him, of course. Then again, he was not entirely human. Like her, he was caught in between.

Dragon and man. Which was he? If he had been hatched, she'd say dragon was his primary self. His true identity. And yet he spent much time as a human, and she had never seen him shift into any other being. Could he? Did he choose this form merely because it was convenient?

Or was he as much man as beast?

She'd never been entirely comfortable with anyone, not even her adopted mother. She'd never felt a part of something, anything, greater than herself. Until she'd found the dragon. Was this where she belonged? With him?

"You asked me once to stay with you, to make love and dance on this mountain for the rest of our lives."

He did not look at her. "That was before you tried to kill me."

She wasn't insulted. "I only meant to keep you on the ground, so Stasio wouldn't realize you were still alive."

"I am not afraid of whoever or whatever your wizard might send after me," Pax growled.

Her wizard. She wished she could dispute that point, but she could not. "I am afraid of those he would send to destroy my family."

He did not argue, so maybe he accepted her argument. That didn't mean he forgave her, of course.

"I am changed," she said softly. "All my life, I have pretended to be human, while inside me the demon simmered, sleeping but never absent. Then I decided to pretend to be entirely demon. I am not that, either. The human in me, the heart my family nurtured, simmered. I must accept that I am both, that I cannot choose one or the other. I am as I am.

"For as long as I can remember, I have been told

I was more powerful than others of my kind, that I was special. I've waited years for my demonic gifts to appear and grow, and of late I have found…abilities. But what if the power I was promised had nothing to do with demonic abilities? What if my ability is to love?"

For a long time they stood there, looking at the world below, thinking of what was to come. Finally, Pax asked, "That sounds pretty, but I have to wonder if you only wish to stay with me because I can feed you without dying."

After all the lies, she could be honest with him now. She had no choice. "I don't think so. I've known life without the hunger. The amulet I told you about, the one my mother made for me, made it possible for me to survive without taking another's life force. I hope she can fashion and bless another, once our task has been completed."

"I have not yet forgiven you."

That *yet* gave her hope in a time where she had thought to know none.

The wind picked up and lifted Pax's long, thick hair. She caught a glimpse of his back and the ridges there, the part of the dragon that never entirely faded. He'd hidden that part of himself from her, with his hair, with his awful, tattered shirt. She crossed the short distance that separated them and placed her fingertips on his spine, tracing the ridges. With that touch, she could see more of him. His pain, his indecision, his anger, his determination.

His love.

He did not like it, but he did love her. Even though she had brought him down; even though she had lied to him from the moment they'd met.

She could tell him, here and now, that she loved him. She'd accepted that love for a while now. But they could not go into battle with the confession hanging between them. She couldn't assure him that she would survive. If she poured out her heart to him and he did the same, her death would be all the more devastating for him.

She was prepared to die, if necessary. If that happened, she wanted him to be free to fly away, to be happy. Even to love again.

But there was something she could say.

"Thank you," she whispered, as she dropped her hand from his back. "Thank you for showing me who I truly am."

CHAPTER 18

Val tried hard not to look at the stand of trees. How many demons waited there? What abilities might they have?

She shifted her stance a bit and pretended to admire the colorful sunset, an enchanting mixture of pink and orange and purple streaking across the sky. Unexpectedly, the sight calmed her. She wasn't one to normally take the time to appreciate something so ordinary, though on occasion one caught her eye. There would be other sunsets, many sunrises, an unending number of flowering trees and summer rains and...

With war so close it seemed that nothing was truly unending. Tomorrow was not promised. For some, this sunset would be the last.

Moments earlier her father had dismounted well short of the wooded area where an ambush awaited, to examine his mount's front hooves with evident displeasure. It would appear to anyone who might be watching that he was concerned for the animal and also annoyed by the delay. They made camp earlier than they'd originally planned, earlier than those who waited in the shadow of the trees ahead might've thought they would.

The attack would have to wait, or else the enemy would have to leave their cover and come to them. They'd be far more exposed than they'd planned. Val and her army would be ready. Were the demons gathered there patient enough to wait until tomorrow?

Could an army of mortal men — with one child among them — ever be ready to face an army of demon daughters? The demons were all young women, perhaps seemingly vulnerable. But they were powerful, each one with their unique gifts. Or curses.

Val reminded herself that none of those they faced in battle would be among the small number of daughters of the Isen Demon who'd chosen to embrace their human selves above the darkness. Those few — far too few — were in hiding, from all she'd heard. And still, knowing that there were some who had managed to deny the darkness gave her hope. For the war. For Columbyana.

Her father walked toward her, a scowl on his face, a hard oatcake grasped in one hand. He handed the food to her and she took it, noting as she did the contrast between her hand and his. His hand was large and hard and scarred. Hers was small, the hand of a child, still.

She did not feel like a child. She never had.

"How many do you expect?" she asked, and then she took a small bite. Her stomach was roiling so viciously that she could not even think of eating much.

"I have no idea. Can't Kitty tell you?"

Not sure, not yet.

Val relayed the message, and then added, "If there is a seer among them, they will know what we're doing."

"That's a possibility."

No seer, Kitty said. *Powerful demons with lightning in their fingertips and supreme strength, one who will fly and two Ksana demons. But none have the sight.*

Again, Val relayed Kitty's words.

"They will wait until it's fully dark to attack," her father said. "We'll be ready for them."

The general's posture changed subtly, and it wasn't long before Val understood why. Cyrus joined them. Her father didn't like the farmer's son much.

"What is my part in the plan?" Cyrus asked.

"You have no part," General Merin snapped. "I will not have my men or my daughter distracted while trying to protect an untrained soldier. Just…" he waved his hand in a dismissive manner. "Hide. Or better yet, leave us. Yes, it would be best if you headed for home now."

Instead of slinking away, as many did when confronted by the general when he was in such a state, Cyrus stood taller. He did not back away, not even an inch. "I'm not leaving without Valora."

"She's not going with you." It was a matter-of-fact statement from a stern father.

"Then here I will stay."

Somehow the two men had gradually moved closer together until they were almost nose to nose. The confrontation had caught the attention of many soldiers who were near enough to hear.

Not that it was necessary to hear to know there was a disagreement going on. Each maintained a stance that spoke of aggression and displeasure. Over her?

Cyrus's hands balled into fists. "I don't understand how a man can willingly send his daughter into battle! She's not much more than a child, and you…"

"Watch your tongue, boy."

Cyrus was not intimidated. "At this moment I don't care about prophecies or destined battles. I don't care how well-trained Valora is, or that she carries a magical sword that apparently speaks to her, or that she's…" His chin seemed to stiffen before he caught his breath and continued, "Or that she's stronger than I will ever be. Danger is upon us, and she should be protected."

Val shifted, trying to place herself between the two men, but she was too late. Her red-faced father moved even closer to Cyrus. "Do you think I like the idea of my daughter going into battle? Do you think I take any pleasure in knowing what's coming for her? Don't you think I want to protect her?"

Cyrus remained calm. "Apparently not."

Kitty began to buzz. Val gasped as her father drew his hand back as if he intended to strike the man who had dared to confront him.

With a sidestep and a squirming motion, Val managed to insert herself between them.

"Double our number," she said.

Both men looked at her. Her father's hand remained raised. "What?"

"The demons, they are double our number. And they're coming. Now."

Pax was glad — relieved, really — to filch a pair of trousers and a linen shirt from a small farm near the foothills. As he'd told Linara, he'd stolen clothing before, when it was necessary. He'd always returned at a later time with better clothes or a bit of coin in repayment, leaving whatever offering he had on a doorstep or on yet another line of drying clothes. This time, he wasn't sure when or if he would return. For the first time, he felt like an actual thief.

The clothes he stole were clean, freshly washed and left drying on a line along with a woman's dress which was as well-worn as the pants and shirt he took. Even though he felt like a thief, he was happy to get out of the dead Caradon's clothes, which were too small and stunk to the heavens.

Linara started to move away, and then she

hesitated, as if she were uncertain about what came next. She stuck a hand into the pocket of her dress pulled out a few pieces of dragonstone, which she dropped to the ground. The stones glimmered, unlike anything that might be found in or near this farm.

She looked at him, and then toward the small house. They saw no sign of life there. The residents were working elsewhere, it seemed, or else hiding from the thieves who might be more than thieves. "A promise that I will return one day with payment of some sort."

A woman who would worry about taking an old shirt and pair of pants without offering compensation could not be evil.

It was just dark, the sun finally gone from the sky, as they walked away from the farm. Linara was in the lead. She did not mind turning her back to him, even though he had not given her his forgiveness. Even though he carried his sword in one hand. He wanted to fly, and probably could, even though he was not entirely healed, but he remained grounded. Hidden. Not for himself, but for Linara's family.

Linara was a demon who had been sent to his home to kill him, but she loved her family. She would sacrifice anything, even him, for them.

And so like it or not, he could forgive her anything.

He tried to remember if he had ever forgiven

anyone. Perhaps he had, at some point during his long lifetime, but no example came to him. Linara had come to his mountain to assassinate him; she had lied; she had stolen his sword. Who could forgive such acts of treachery? She'd used his own sword to bring him down. No matter what her reasons had been...she had attacked him as no other ever had.

And yet, he still thought of a future with her. She was no dragon; she was not his mate, and yet he could imagine too well just the two of them, settling on the mountain which was now behind them, or on any other. The world had many mountains, many caves and ponds and hills. Those mountains were lush and harsh, cold and warm, barren and filled with life. No matter which one they chose, they could have everything they needed. Sex. Laughter. A home. Not a home like any Linara had ever known, but a home just the same.

If they both survived this war, if she would have him, if he could...

Linara held up one hand as she came to an abrupt stop. He stopped, too, wondering what she had heard that he had not.

"My sisters, they attack."

He moved closer. "The village? How close are we?"

"Not the village." She turned to the east. "We're too far away, but...they need us. They need help."

And he had just been thinking of sharing a

lifetime with her! "I have no intention of helping your damned sisters."

Linara spun on him. "Not them," she whispered hotly. "We need to help those who are being attacked by my sisters." She took a deep breath. "They are too far away, but you can take me there. With flight, we can get there in time. Fly low and save your flame."

All her life, Val had known she was meant for this. That didn't make her first battle any easier.

Demons came, some running, more than one flying. The soldiers did not hesitate. For some of them, this wasn't their first encounter with an enemy who appeared to be a helpless female. The others adapted quickly. It was that or death.

Soldiers fell, but so did demons. They were not invincible, but they were fearsome adversaries. Some fought, as the men did, with weapons made by human hands. Others sent lightning and fire hurtling through the air. Sometimes the magical weapons found their intended target, but often they did not. The demons were powerful, but they were not trained fighters, and changing their plan of attack had rattled a few of them.

It could be said that they suffered from overconfidence.

Val was a target; she noted that several of the demons set their sights on her as soon as they were close. They worked their way toward her, leaping with grace, all but flying, moving faster than was normal and cutting down the soldiers that got in their way.

As one hurtled toward Val, hands like claws raised in the air, Cyrus — wielding only a long knife — threw himself in front of her. The demon never took her eyes from Val; she simply tossed Cyrus aside like a rag doll Val's youngest sister liked to sleep with.

As Val watched Cyrus fly, something happened to her. Her focus intensified, and she felt a new strength flow through her. Everything around her was suddenly washed in the colors of the rainbow. The approaching demon paused and then stumbled, before continuing.

Princess, Kitty whispered.

She is not...

That is the name this Ksana gave herself, when Stasio found her. She came before you. She was once...

There was no more time for words, magical or otherwise. Val lifted her sword and swung.

Princess was fast. She ducked and spun. And she smiled. When she turned her head, Val saw a scar on the demon's neck.

Normally, the demons didn't scar. The wound must've been deep.

Instead of turning to Val, Princess leaped to the place where Cyrus lay on the ground. Dead? No, he stirred. Princess looked at Val, then smiled widely as she dropped to her knees and lowered her mouth to Cyrus'.

Val pushed past a wounded man. The battling soldier would be fine; he did not need her. Cyrus did need her. She spared a glance for her father, who was holding his own, as were most of his men. When she reached Cyrus, she raised a booted foot and kicked Princess off of him. The demon, surprised by Val's strength, flew off the body and landed on her rear end in the dirt.

And then she laughed. Val wanted to look to Cyrus, to make sure he was still alive, that the Ksana had not drained him in the short amount of time they'd been touching. She didn't dare take her eyes from Princess.

"They said you were strong," Princess said as she leaped to her feet and brushed the dirt from her skirt. "You might be harder to kill than they…"

An ear-splitting roar from the near distance grabbed everyone's attention. Val turned, and so did Princess. So did they all. For a moment, the battle came to a standstill. The night stopped.

Val blinked once, to make sure she wasn't hallucinating.

A dragon, flying low to the ground, approached with great speed. A woman rode upon its back, and she held a sword high. It was a sight Val had never thought to see, something out of a bedtime story or a myth of earlier days. The dragon and the woman

212 | Linda Winstead Jones

crashed into the battle. Clawed feet dug into the
ground and sent dirt and grass flying. Oh, the size
of the beast!

Ksana, Kitty whispered, and Val's heart stopped.
Her small army had a chance against the demons
alone, but they could not defeat a dragon. When it
spat fire...

One of the demons who had the gift of flight
rose into the air and drifted toward the intruders.
For a better look, or did she simply want a word with
the woman on the dragon's back a woman who was,
apparently, one of their own? She moved past the
dragon's head, the shirt of her simple gray dress
trailing behind her like fog on an early morning.
The beast turned its head, but still, there was no fire.

Reinforcements. How could they fight a
dragon?

The flying demon was shocked when the
woman on the dragon rose up, swung the massive
sword, and took her head. Val was shocked, too. So
were the other demons, who panicked and ran
toward the trees. Even Princess retreated.

The dragon, which was beautiful in flight, Val
had to admit — even more beautiful now that she
knew it was on the right side of the battle — rose
high, then dropped and turned, swooping overhead
and creating a warm breeze. A massive tail, thick
and long and powerful, a weapon all its own,
whipped in the air. The swinging tail made a
whistling sound, much like a stormy wind in the

trees. Now behind the retreating demons, the dragon spit forth a white hot flame they could not outrun.

They were demons, but they screamed like women as they died. They were aflame, even the Ksana Princess who had tried to kill Cyrus. Val wasn't sorry, she couldn't be sorry, but for a long moment, she closed her eyes against the horrifying sight.

She did not stay in that position long. She turned away from the burning demons, dropping to her knees beside Cyrus. Kitty fell a short distance to the dirt. The sword gave an indignant but short-lived howl as Val placed her trembling hands on Cyrus' pale cheeks. His eyes were closed. His lips were parted and pale.

"Please be alive," she whispered. "Please, don't die."

CHAPTER 19

Linara clung to the spikes on the dragon's back as he drifted down, slowly and gracefully moving closer to the ground. She was sharply aware that the spikes shifted into a spine when Pax became man. The color and harshness, the strength and the beauty, were a part of him no matter his form.

Man or beast, he was always Pax.

He lowered himself fully; his talons dug into the grass. That done, he dipped down a bit more to allow her to slip off his back. It wasn't easy, it was a long way to the ground, but she managed. With Pax's sword and the borrowed clothes in hand, she dropped to the blessed earth. Her head spun and her knees went weak. She resisted the urge to drop to her knees and kiss the grass.

One would think riding a dragon would be lots of fun, but she had been terrified the entire time. The dragon moved fast, and far off the ground, and to her knowledge, Pax was not accustomed to a rider. Would he let her fall? Accidentally or on purpose? He could, and with all that had happened between them she couldn't blame him. Not entirely.

He had not let her fall, and that was encouraging.

By the time a small contingent of soldiers reached them, Pax had shifted and was stepping into his trousers. The shirt, he merely tossed over his shoulder.

Perhaps he wanted the cool air on his skin to ease the heat the dragon created. Then again, he had no more reason to hide his back from her, or from anyone else present. They had all seen his true self. They knew he was the dragon.

Linara faced the men. She smiled a little as she recognized the one in the lead.

"General Merin," she said as calmly as possible. "It's good to see you again."

He narrowed his dark eyes. "Do I know you?"

"We met once, years ago, when my parents were visiting Arthes. I was younger then, of course. I have changed. You have not." She stepped forward and offered her hand. "Linara Varden."

He took her hand and shook it, briefly, but his suspicion did not fade. "As I recall, Sophie and Kane Varden took you in as an infant. You are..." He could not say it, but she could.

"Ksana, yes. I am a Ksana demon."

The men behind backed away. Some of them gasped and drew their swords. She was not surprised.

"But I assure you, general; I am on your side. I believe my friend and I have just proven that."

She looked to the camp behind the soldiers. A small fire still burned. Men had been injured, and a

216 | Linda Winstead Jones

handful of others had remained behind to tend to them. "I can help with the wounded, if you will allow me to do so."

General Merin appeared to be resigned. He'd fought in many battles in his lifetime, but none quite like this one. "You and your friend saved our asses, Miss Varden." He cast a slightly suspicious glance Pax's way. "You can do whatever you'd like."

Cyrus opened one eye to see a pretty fair-haired woman bending over him. His heart thudded, hard. It was her, the one who had attacked Val and then him. The one who had kissed him. That kiss had hurt, but he had not been able to turn away.

The demon was back to finish what she'd started. Killing him.

She touched his face with gentleness, and he realized with a touch of relief this was a different pretty blonde. His vision remained fuzzy, he was dizzy, but no, this was not *that* demon. The one who had kissed him. Still, he struggled against her touch as much as he could. This had to be another demon...

"Be still," a familiar voice whispered.

Cyrus turned his head, a little. It was Val, kneeling beside him. She seemed to be unharmed, and she was calm. Why was she calm?

Her eyes were so bright, so filled with color. Not her usual green, but every color you might imagine.

She...she glowed, washed in all those colors; she lit the night like a cluster of rainbow stars. Must be his injury that made him see things so skewed. Maybe he had hit his head and was hallucinating.

"I'm going to marry you, one day," he said. He hadn't planned to tell Val of his plans, not so soon, but the confession erupted from his mouth without any thought.

Her father must be near. That was the general's usual grunt of displeasure Cyrus heard.

Val's eyes widened, and the color shifted from all those rainbow colors to the green he preferred. "Hush, now. You're delirious. You must've hit your head."

"I did, but that's not why I said what I said." He wanted to tell her everything, while he could. "I dreamed we would marry, when we're both older. The same way I dreamed of Kitty's scabbard, I dreamed of us. The images were foggy, though, as if there was something in the way. A film that covered everything. I think we both have to survive this war before..."

Val looked surprised and uneasy. She squirmed. Then she pursed her lips a moment before saying, "You need to rest. This nice lady is going to heal you, but you must be quiet while she works."

The "nice lady" was a demon. Cyrus saw that clearly, even though he was not asleep. Normally he only knew things he should not in his dreams. Maybe the head injury had caused some confusion in the gifts he had never wanted. The woman looked at him, hard. She had striking blue eyes like ice in the sky. Her hair was fair, her skin flawless, her features formed what any man might call perfect beauty. But she paled next to Valora, with her wild dark hair and her expressive eyes.

"This film," the pretty demon said as she laid her hands on him, "the one in your dreams. What does it look like?"

Cyrus had to think a moment, to recall the images that had come to him so often as he slept. "Fire," he finally whispered, seeing it in his mind more clearly than before. Seeing it as if it were real. And near. "Not just any fire, but massive, curling flames with the power to wipe out anything in its path." He had not realized that before, but he knew it now.

The demon sighed. "Dragonfire, perhaps?"

Cyrus would have popped up as he heard the words, if she'd let him. His heart pounded as if it was trying to break through his chest. The pretty demon was stronger than she looked. She held him in place. "Yes," he said. "Dragonfire."

Her decision had been made the moment she'd joined General Merin and his soldiers in fighting the attackers. If Stasio knew, if he had seen what happened through the eyes of the demons the way he had so often seen through hers...

She had no time to waste. If Stasio realized what she had done, Linara's mother was in grave and immediate danger.

The boy was healed, as much as was possible given her distraction. He'd live, at least for now. His injuries from this battle would not keep him from his destined marriage, but she couldn't guarantee that nothing else would. There would likely be many obstacles beyond this battle.

Linara popped up, brushing dust off her skirt as she turned to look for Pax. He stood alone outside the circle of light from the campfire. The soldiers were leery of him, after watching him shift from dragon to man, and besides, they had their hands full caring for their own. Remarkably, only two had died in battle. There were a number of injuries, though.

She ran toward Pax. "We must go. Now."

"Where?"

"The village. Stasio. If he saw…"

Pax nodded and began to remove his clothes. "Your mother."

Linara nodded. She ignored the first shouted wait, but she could not ignore the second, as it came with a firm hand on her shoulder.

She spun to face the young man she had just healed. Cyrus, they said his name was.

"You can't go," Cyrus said. His face was pale; he was far from well.

"I don't have any choice."

He shook his head. "Finally, they are together. One born…"

"One hatched, one created," Linara barked. "I am so sick and tired of hearing those words, over and over and…"

"They will be necessary to defeat the dark wizard. His defeat will be the beginning of the end for the demon daughters." His pale blue eyes seemed to sparkle.

"You're a wizard?" she asked. He'd felt entirely ordinary when she'd healed him.

Cyrus shook his head. "I don't know. I used to have dreams that came true, but now it seems that my head is filled with knowledge. I can't make sense of it all, but I do know we can't separate them. Not now. They might never again be together, and they must be together. They must."

The girl, a child, General Merin's daughter Val, stood close behind Cyrus now, a gleaming sword in one hand. It wasn't just firelight that made the sword gleam, it was the crystal grip.

Dragonstone.

"I assume Val is the born."

Cyrus nodded.

"And the created?"

Val held her sword high, and the gleam grew to the point where it was almost impossible to look directly at it.

"Fine," Pax snapped. "No need to be a nag. I heard you the first time."

Confused, Linara turned to face him. "I didn't say a word."

"No, but she did." He pointed to Val. "You didn't hear?"

"No, I…"

Ahh, it hadn't been Val, it had been the sword. The living being that had been forged into a weapon, the third piece of the puzzle.

Val smiled. "I'm so glad someone besides me can hear her!"

Pax began to shift, and everyone — wounded or not — stopped what they were doing to watch. It was a magnificent and rare sight, one only a handful of people would ever see.

When he was dragon, he lowered himself to the ground so that Val, sword in hand, could climb upon his back. She made much quicker and easier work of it than Linara had done.

A young girl sitting atop a fire-spitting beast, sword in hand, an unexpected smile on her face. Now that was a magnificent sight.

"Stop!" Linara shouted. "I'm going with you."

Cyrus trailed her as she ran to collect Pax's sword. "You can't go. I see it clearly. They will fly into the village, just the three of them, as the sun is rising. That will be the beginning of the end for the daughters of the Isen Demon; that is how it must happen. You are not supposed to be there."

She would not give up so easily. "They can leave me nearby before they fly in to do what has to be

222 | Linda Winstead Jones

done."

"Stay…"

Linara collected the massive sword, Pax's sword, and spun around. Cyrus had to dance out of the way in order to escape the swing of the blade. "I will not stay."

She met Pax's eye and reached into his mind in the only way she knew how. *We know what must be done. If you can't burn Stasio, I will take his head.*

The massive dragon dipped his big, beautiful head in agreement.

CHAPTER 20

Until he'd flown Linara into battle, Pax had never before experienced the feel of a human upon his back. It was annoying at first, as if a parasite had attached itself to his scales. He instinctively wanted to shake off that which should not be there, but he had not.

And now he carried two. A woman and a child.

And me, Kitty said, slipping too easily into his mind.

He gave thanks that his own sword didn't talk. After that, Kitty remained silent.

In short order, he could cover ground it would take days or even weeks for a man to walk. If Linara's mother was in danger, they had to hurry, and he had to make sure they weren't seen too soon. He stayed low to the ground, and he kept his fire contained. For now.

He swerved sharply to avoid a stand of trees, and Linara held on tighter than before. She gasped and her heart raced. The girl Val laughed. That one had been made for riding dragons.

He could deposit Linara here, far from the village, where she would be safe when the battle that was to come started. But safety was not her concern, nor was it his. In darkness, he flew around the village and set down on a narrow section of rock. He looked down upon the collection of plain buildings. If not for a few soldiers standing watch, it would look like any other small village.

Sword in hand, Linara clumsily climbed over one side and slid off his back. He heard her stumble a little, but she did not fall. He turned his head to look at her.

She looked deeply into one eye, placed a hand on his scaly face, and said, "I wanted to wait, but I have to confess, in case I don't see you again...I love you. Man or beast, lover or dragon, I love you. Take care of yourself."

He loved her, too, but did not have the words. Not at this moment.

And then she was back to business. "Give me half an hour to get into position before you attack."

"Half an hour?" Val snapped. "Does he have an internal clock of some kind, because I sure don't."

Linara looked to the east. "As the first sliver of the sun shows on the horizon, show them what it means to truly be at war."

With that, Pax rose into the air.

Linara watched them fly away, in darkness, low to the ground. They were a magnificent sight, these prophesied three. They would survive this day; she knew it. Val would return to her Cyrus, and one day, in a few years, they'd marry. Pax would return to his mountain, or to another mountain, where he would continue to cook and eat the worst of men. Or women.

She had no idea what happened to a magical sword when its purpose had been served.

And she had no confidence at all that she herself would survive.

Linara scrambled down the hill, careful to make no sound even though she was not directly behind the village. At this time of the morning, the demons and soldiers slept. Most of them, at least. There were a handful of guards, but the army was overly confident. They had demons on their side, and so they knew no fear.

If Stasio slept, this would be the time. If her mother was there, somewhere...

She wouldn't think of that, not now. Find Stasio. Find Sophie Fyne Varden. End this, one way or another.

Very soon, the landscape began to look familiar. Ahead, through the trees, she saw the rear of the tavern. All was quiet there, at this hour.

She stumbled a bit, tripping over her own two feet it seemed. She caught herself without taking a tumble, and looked to see what had caused her to lose her footing.

There was no light to speak of, no reason for the amulet to sparkle as it did. And yet there it was, calling to her. She had not seen it since the night

226 | Linda Winstead Jones

she'd ripped it from her neck and tossed it away. It had been here, all this time, waiting for her to return and claim it. Linara almost gleefully snatched the charm from the ground and dropped it in her pocket.

And she was more positive than ever that her mother was here, and still alive.

She walked forward, more determined than ever, and she whispered, "I'm coming."

Stasio paced the small room, glancing only occasionally at the woman who was bound to a wooden chair in the center of the room. Sophie Fyne Varden was unnervingly calm. He could kill her for that, and might, eventually, but she still served a purpose.

She would bring Linara back to him.

Having Sophie here had cost him dearly. Only one of the four soldiers he'd sent to collect the witch had returned with her. The other three had, one after the other, attempted to help the woman they'd been assigned to kidnap. She'd worked her way under their skin, thanks to her magic. Their chivalry had been rewarded with death at the hand of one of their compatriots. Thank goodness the last soldier had been dark enough to resist her white magic long enough to deliver her.

He had watched the night's disastrous battle through the eyes of two of his strongest girls, but what he had seen had been maddeningly disjointed and vague. They had died, he knew that much, in dragonfire. Fire from the dragon Linara had been sent to kill. She'd failed in that task, but had she assisted the dragon or had she been fighting against it?

He could not trust her. She'd shown him the dragon's death; a man's death. She had made him believe…

He could no longer see through her eyes; she had learned to block him. But she wasn't dead. No, she couldn't be dead.

The woman, who thankfully did not speak too much, surprised him by saying, "You should release me now."

He looked at her, annoyed by her calm demeanor, by her strength and beauty that had survived too many years.

"And why should I do that?"

"My husband will be here soon, and he won't come alone. I can feel his nearness from here. They've traveled through the night." She tsked, and lifted her eyebrows in a chastising manner. "He's annoyed with you."

Stasio was pretty *annoyed* himself. He planted his feet in front of the chair, and leaned down to place his face close to hers. He didn't like it; being near to her made him intensely uncomfortable in his own skin. But he forced a smile. He whispered, "When he gets here, I will skin him alive. I'll let you live long enough to watch."

She was no longer calm. Her blue eyes flashed. Her fair hair — more gray than blond now, but in a silvery way that reminded him of Linara — lifted a little, as if a gentle wind rushed around her. "If you lay a finger on Kane, you will regret it."

Stasio scoffed, he turned away before the witch could see the fear those simple words ignited in him.

Perhaps he should have left Linara's mother alone.

Unfortunately for him, that knowledge came too late.

He drew the dagger he had taken to wearing and held it before the witch's face. "You will bring Linara to me, and I will kill her for her betrayal."

Sophie's eyes flashed with anger. "You well know a Ksana is hard to kill. You'd be better off to let me and my daughter go."

He moved the blade back and forth, experiencing a surge of confidence. "Do you think I would surround myself with demons without having a way to end their lives? This blade will destroy the heart of any demon daughter. I fashioned it, and the dark magic within, myself."

He expected another flash of anger, but Sophie remained calm. She almost smiled. "My daughter does not have a demon heart."

***

The sky turned gray, but the sun had not yet shown itself; not even a golden sliver was visible on the horizon, but...soon.

Linara crept along the edge of the tavern, staying in the dark shadows as she listened. Stasio didn't sleep much. He seemed to think sleep was a waste of time, that there were better things to be done with his hours. Fortunately all but a handful of posted guards slept at this hour. If she listened. If she tried very hard...

And there it was. A whisper. A voice only she could hear. No, *voices*.

One of them was her mother's.

There was no time to be cautious. Soon the sun would arrive, and Pax would come soaring in, fire blazing. What would Stasio do then? He would realize that Linara had failed, and he would kill his hostage.

The faint whisper led her to a house three doors from the tavern. It was not a place Stasio had called home in the past. Was he hiding from her? Was he afraid to be found?

Linara peeked through an uncovered window near the narrow front door. Her heart stopped for a moment when she saw her mother there, tied to a chair, foolishly smiling and arguing with Stasio. She blinked twice. Her mother...glowed. She was surrounded by a powerful white light. Did Stasio see that light, or was he blind to it?

The wizard stood apart from her, thank the

heavens. If he had been too near Sophie, if he had been threatening her, Linara's next move would've been a bit trickier.

She opened the door and stepped inside.

She was riding a dragon. A dragon! The wind blew Val's hair behind her, pulling at it. That wind whipped her clothing; it stung her exposed skin. And it was wonderful. It was all wonderful.

The dragon — Pax — seemed not to tire of flying. They could've set down under cover of darkness and waited for sunrise, but instead, they flew toward the mountain in the distance, low and fast, then turned toward the village, increasing their speed with every passing moment.

Val gave a moment's thought to Cyrus and what he'd said after the battle. Married? She did like him. She liked him a lot. And he had been a steadfast companion during the journey to bring her to this place. Sometimes she looked at him and got butterflies in her stomach, but she was young, and he was young, and who knew what the coming years might bring?

She could easily imagine Cyrus being a part of her coming years...

Since finding Kitty, Val and the magical sword had been connected. Mentally, spiritually, they were, on occasion, one. It was that way now with the three of them. Val dismissed musings of a future with Cyrus. Three minds melded. Three souls entwined. One born, one hatched, one created. They had one purpose.

Stop the demons. Save the world.

I am ready.

The first sliver of an orange sun peeked over the horizon.

It is time.

CHAPTER 21

It was perhaps the first time she'd ever surprised Stasio. He jumped when the door swung open, spinning around to glare at Linara, wide-eyed.

"You didn't see me coming, did you?" she asked, keeping her voice calm.

He looked into her eyes, and then at the sword she carried. Pax's sword.

His surprise was short-lived. "I told you what would happen if you dared to disobey me." He brandished a plain but deadly looking dagger and danced quickly to Sophie's side. In an instant, the blade was at her throat, but he did not draw blood.

Perhaps he realized that a living Sophie was all the leverage he had.

"I knew you would come," Sophie said in a low, calm voice.

"Mother, please..." Linara began.

"When you were a child, an infant even, I dreamed of this moment."

Linara kept her eyes on Stasio. "And how does it end?"

Sophie knit her eyebrows together. "I'm afraid I never saw that clearly. There's too much still to be decided." She smiled. "But not your heart, daughter.

Your heart is strong and good. That was decided long ago."

Stasio was not moved by the words. "A human heart will be easier to destroy."

Sophie remained calm. "You are wrong, wizard. There is nothing stronger than the human heart."

Something about the tone of her voice disturbed Stasio. Linara could see it. He responded with a bitter, "You do not know what your *daughter* has done, witch. She's a killer. A demon. And though she might not yet accept it, she is mine. I will have her at my side, or I will see her dead."

His grip on the knife changed. Blood bloomed there, on Sophie's fine, pale throat.

And the sun rose.

They swooped into the village, startling the soldiers who had been guarding the perimeter. As if they could keep a dragon at bay. Val held Kitty high. The grip glowed so brightly it should have burned her palm, but it did not.

Pax let loose his fire, striking down the soldiers, one and then another. And another.

More soldiers — male and female — poured from the houses and businesses of the village, drawn by the screams of their compatriots. There were a lot of them, more than Val had expected there would be. How much fire did Pax possess? Was it an endlessly available ability, or would it...

Ah, all she had to do was tap into the power of three, and she knew. The fire was not endless. He had never before faced such a large number of opponents, but he knew he did not have enough fire to kill them all.

His attention was diverted, and Val's eyes were drawn to that which had alarmed him. Linara stepped from a building near the center of the village, a man wearing a black robe behind her. They were both armed, she with a sword, he with a knife that seemed to be wrapped in a dark fog. There was magic in that dagger, and it was not of the good sort.

Stasio.

Val had not heard the name, but Pax knew it, and therefore so did she. He was a bad man, a dark wizard, the self-appointed leader of these misguided and evil and lost soldiers who made up the army he led.

Goodness, it was as if she could feel the lift in Linara's heart as she watched them fly around and drop again, as if she were washed in the half-demon's hope and love.

Ewww. *Let's stick to the battle, shall we?*

Pax dropped to let loose his fire again, as Stasio and Linara battled in the midst of it all.

Linara stepped back and then back again. Stasio matched her step for step. Her mother was wounded but would live, as long as Stasio died. As long as she won this battle. She could not afford to lose.

Pax and Val could take care of the soldiers, but Stasio was hers. She had to end him, and now.

In close quarters, Pax's sword was all but useless. Every time Linara tried to retreat and lift the sword, Stasio moved with her. He knew, as she did, that with a bit of distance and one lucky swing, he'd be dead.

Her only chance was to do battle with him outside this small room. She turned and ran through the door. He followed, leaving his prisoner to pursue what he most wanted. Her. Linara spun to face him, and in spite of herself, she smiled. One way or another, this ended today.

He moved quickly, grabbing Linara's arm before she could swing the sword, spinning her about and pushing her against the wall of the building where her wounded mother remained prisoner. Not for long.

With a strong hand and a bit of magic, he stripped the sword away. It was ripped from her hand and sent flying, landing in the dirt and skidding away an incredible distance.

Sophie had said Linara's heart had been decided long ago, but Linara was not so sure. When she healed, when she helped, the white light grew. When she used her demon's powers to hurt, the darkness took hold. Did that make her heart stronger or weaker? Was a human heart, as her

236 | Linda Winstead Jones

mother said, incredibly strong?

A stream of white hot dragonfire to her right took out five soldiers who'd been advancing, perhaps to assist their leader. Linara wanted to look at Pax, to thank him, but she didn't dare.

Stasio needed no help. He held the knife against her breast, there above her heart. She'd be hard to kill, but death could come for her. That dark dagger could easily destroy her heart, whether that heart was filled with darkness or light.

"I had so hoped for more from you," Stasio said. He sounded like a disappointed father, a stern teacher whose student had failed an assignment.

Linara lifted her face and looked him in the eye. The morning sun continued to rise, and it sent a shaft across his face. By the light of day he looked...ordinary. Plain. A man, and nothing more.

"Kiss me," she whispered.

"I am no fool..."

"You are nothing but a fool. A fool possessed of a bit of magic. An ambitious fool, to be sure, but still..."

"If I destroy your heart with this blade, you will die."

"I know."

His lips thinned and tightened. His eyes...his eyes were dead, as they always had been. "So why do you taunt me?"

Because in the end, her death would mean something. But only if she could take him with her.

"What makes you think you are like ordinary men? No other man can withstand the kiss of a Ksana demon, but you...you are stronger than other men, are you not? I kissed Pax, and he lives."

"He's a dragon."

"You're a wizard." And he had always wanted her. He'd wanted to touch her, to have her. Was she his weakness? Could she use that weakness against him?

His knife shifted as she forced herself up. It sliced into her flesh, just barely into her heart. The intense pain surprised her, but she held on. She possessed an undeniable strength, as well as a determination to see this done. Her chin came up, her head tilted, and she clasped her mouth to his.

Once she had him, he could not let go. He tried; she felt the struggle within him, the desire to live. His essence flowed into her, it fed her. Was it enough? Could she survive? She was willing to die, but like Stasio, she wanted to live.

With a burst of brute force, a final effort to save himself, he buried the blade even deeper in her heart. She almost fell back, away from him, but she held on tight. He was hers, now. Now and forever.

He released the knife, but it stayed within her, within her heart. It hurt; it burned; it sucked the life from her the way she sucked the life from him. He fell into her and the blade slipped deeper. Who would die first? Who would win this battle of dark magic?

Linara felt the blood dripping down her torso. It was warm, like human blood. Her good heart was destroyed, or nearly so. She did not have much time left. Enough? Was it enough?

Stasio tried to scream, but he could not. And then he was gone, dust in the wind, a pile of bones and robes that stunk of darkness and sweat and desperation. Linara's legs went out from under her, and she dropped to the ground, her back to the wall, her vision going. Before her, soldiers continued to come. So many, more than she had imagined would be here on this morning.

Pax landed in the center of the village. His weight made the ground shake. There was no more fire, but he swung his tail and took out six soldiers at once, as an arrow found its mark in his neck. He howled, but not in pain.

He howled for her.

Stasio was dead, but they were going to lose the battle. She'd been so sure they would win. They were destined to win. And really, the war was over. Without Stasio the rebel troops wouldn't hold together. Without his protection, the Isen demon's daughters would be weakened and separated. But right now, in this village, there too many soldiers.

Linara expected to die, then and there, but she did not. Her vision began to return, if not her strength. More arrows aimed at the dragon found their mark; a brave soldier moved in and swung his sword at Pax's throat. He was ended when Val jumped from her perch and took his head with Kitty.

She was glad Pax had Val and Kitty. They would all survive, somehow. They had to.

Linara tried to stand, but she could not. She'd lost too much blood.

She reached out to touch Pax's mind with her own. *I love you. I never expected to love anyone, but I love you.*

The dragon looked at her with eyes on fire. The words she initially heard from him were those of a dragon, harsh and foreign but filled with emotion. With a great effort on his part, he spoke to her in words she could understand. *Tell me again when this battle is over.*

They were losing this fight. In spite of her earlier confidence for Pax and Val, she suspected they would all soon be dead. They were outnumbered. They had struck too soon.

Now Val was surrounded, a little girl wielding a gleaming sword outnumbered by leering, evil men who would not think twice about cutting her down. So much for prophecy! So much for winning! They had sacrificed everything...

The soldiers came out of nowhere, with battle cries and weapons raised. At first, Linara thought they were reinforcements for Stasio's men, that they were even more outnumbered.

She was wrong.

Hope made her damaged heart beat. She might have smiled, if she'd been able. She saw it so clearly. Pax and Val had not attacked too soon; they had arrived just in time.

The newly arrived army was made up entirely of descendants of the Fyne witches. Old and young, most touched with magic but some not, they came from all directions. There were witches and wizards who wielded their swords and their magic. Anwyn men and women, shifters who were fearsome opponents in any battle. A creature much like Pax flew in. The Firebird.

They were joined by skilled soldiers from the Circle of Bacwyr, men who were all but impossible to defeat sword to sword.

Her family. Her brothers and sisters and cousins. Her aunts and uncles.

A man left the battle and ran toward her.

Her father.

Kane Varden dropped down, studying her wound with worry etched on his still-handsome face. "Juliet is close behind us. She will heal you."

She didn't think that was possible, not now, but she smiled weakly.

Her father's face paled a little. "Your mother?"

"Alive and well." If Sophie's sisters were nearby, the small injury Stasio had inflicted upon the youngest Fyne witch would be healed with a touch and a few words. Linara didn't think her own injury would be healed so easily, if at all.

She crooked her head to indicate the door at her side. "Mama's tied up in there. Go to her." Before he could stand, Linara reached out and snagged his wrist, holding on as tightly as she could. "I love you, Papa."

He looked puzzled. She'd never been one for a declaration of any kind. "Love you, too, sweetie." He patted her hand. "You'll be fine."

Linara closed her eyes and drifted away. Fine? She didn't think so.

CHAPTER 22

Memories of long ago battles, images, and powerful scents filled Pax's mind. If dragons were capable of creating endless fire, they could not be defeated. So many others of his kind would not have been destroyed by humans and their weapons.

In past battles, the dragons had been stronger, faster, more lethal than their opponents, and yet they had been all but eliminated. Now, as in the past, there were too many humans, and they kept coming. On and on, without end, they came. Kill one, and ten more arrived to take his place.

Pax's fire died, and he knew from experience that it would not reignite before nightfall. Soon he fought with his talons and his tail, but every piercing arrow, every slash of a sword, weakened him. He could fly away and save himself; there was time. But he did not. Linara fought her own battle, with a man in a dark robe. She was demon. She would survive. She did not need him.

He watched as she sucked the life from the man she fought. No, she did not need him, she never had and she never would. He did not see the knife in her heart, not until she fell.

A blade alone would not kill her. She should

pluck that dagger from her chest and heal quickly, but she did not. She was defeated, fading.

And then she slipped into his head, in that way she had. She spoke to him as only she could. Why did she tell him of her love now? It sounded, to his mind, like a dying confession. She could not die. He would not allow it.

He tried to make his way to her, but there were too many soldiers around him, and he was growing weaker with each breath. He lifted his head and howled.

When the others came — so many, so many humans — he knew the battle was done for. They were outnumbered, and without his fire they were at a great disadvantage. Linara, the child Val, they would not last much longer. In a way he had not expected, he grieved for them. They should have enjoyed long lives, filled with love and laughter.

He did not mourn his own death or regret any of the choices he had made. He'd had a long life, and there had been moments of love and laughter. At this moment it did not matter that he'd never found the mate he'd been promised.

The prophecy about one hatched had obviously been wrong. So was his mother's promise.

Pax heard a familiar scream and turned his gaze to the skies. The Firebird — one like him and yet not — flew overhead. Her fire had not been extinguished.

To his surprise, the newcomers fought not with

244 | Linda Winstead Jones

the demons and their swordsmen, but against them. As soldiers were drawn away from him, Pax found a burst of strength. He used the weapons that remained; his talons and his tail. When Val was threatened from behind by a sword-bearing half-demon who attacked while screaming at the top of her lungs, Pax grabbed the vile woman, piercing her heart in the process.

Some of the demons were hard to kill. This one was not.

Val smiled at him and nodded, and their thoughts melded for a moment.

Thanks.

We have help.

I noticed.

Pax spared a glance for Linara, who should be recovered and standing by now. She was not.

And then the battle, which was quickly turning in their favor, resumed. A seasoned soldier broke from their ranks and ran to Linara. Would he know she was not like the others? Would he try to finish her off? Pax sent a warning to Linara, but they did not connect. She was too weak.

The soldier dipped down and took her hand in his. She spoke to him. Of course, these were her people. This was her army.

The man Linara had spoken with left her and stepped into the building she leaned against. How could he leave her? How could he abandon her when she was in such pain? He saw the pain on her and in her. He saw it all around her, in an aura he had come to know too well.

That aura was fading.

He roared again, and though he was not sure he could survive the shift to his human form with all the wounds he sported, he called upon that gift and began to shrink in upon himself.

A dragon could not hold a dying woman in his arms.

Linara closed her eyes and began to drift. Body and soul, she felt light. Untethered. Free.

A voice pulled her down to earth. "No, no, no."

She opened one eye and Pax was there. Pax the man, not Pax the dragon. He was naked and wounded and covered with blood. And as always, she loved simply looking at him. He was extraordinary.

He sat beside her and pulled her onto his lap. There was so much blood. His and hers, but mostly hers. That blood flowed freely from her heart. Her good heart; the heart Pax loved, whether he would admit to it or not.

"We will fix you," he said.

She rested her head against his chest. "And how will we do that? My heart was shredded by a magical dagger. There's not much I can't come back from, but..."

"If magic injured you, then magic will heal you."

"I don't think…"

"We will find a way."

She knew him well. He was sure that if he insisted, if he believed hard enough, she would survive.

Linara pulled her knees in, curled up in his lap. She liked it here, no matter the circumstance. "I love you," she said.

"Stop saying that!" he growled.

"You're supposed to say, 'I love you, too.' It's the expected human response. Even if you don't love me, I'm dying. You could pretend."

"We're not human."

"We're kind of human." She looked at him and smiled. "I'm glad I didn't kill you."

"I'm glad I didn't kill you, too."

Her eyes fluttered closed. "See? That wasn't so hard."

"Open your eyes," he commanded.

"It's too hard," she whispered.

"Try, for me."

She did. He opened his mouth to say something, maybe to tell her that he did love her, but he was interrupted by a voice from above.

"Kane, who is this large, naked man, and why is he holding our daughter so tightly?"

Pax looked up, blinked, held his breath.

Linara's parents stood there, side by side. They

were both of an age, which showed in a few wrinkles and their gray hair, but they were fit and healthy. They'd had a long life, but they were not yet done.

Pax's voice was a growl as he whispered, "Save her, please."

The bed beneath her was soft; the blanket over her body warm. Pax no longer held her, and she did not feel the seep of her life force running from her body, from her heart. Linara opened one eye, then the other.

Of course. There was no other explanation for her survival.

She had never thought to see the Fyne sisters reunited. They lived a good distance apart, and they were all aging. Well, but aging.

Her mother looked worried. Aunt Juliet smiled kindly, while Isadora glared. She looked royally pissed. As always.

"Thank goodness," Sophie said, as she placed a hand on Linara's forehead. "It's been three days! I thought you'd never wake."

Three days? Three *days*? "Where's Pax?" The words croaked from her, harsh and far softer than she had planned.

"Your dragon is fine," Juliet said in a calm voice. "He needed a bit of work himself, but he took to it well. He's with the men." There was a softening to her words, and to her eyes.

"What of the war?"

Sophie tsked, "We'll have no talk of war, not until you're completely healed."

Linara's still-mending heart sank. If the news had been good, her mother would've told her more.

Isadora tsked herself. "There's no reason not to tell."

"She doesn't need the worry, not yet," Sophie whispered, as if Linara might not be able to hear.

"Good news is not a worry, it's a relief."

Sophie pursed her lips, before saying, "I don't like talk of war, not ever."

Isadora caught Linara's eye. "The battle here turned the tide. Stasio's death was no small part of that." She nodded, perhaps in respect or thanks. "There have been smaller battles across the country, but it seems that the demon daughters have...lost heart." She smiled. "The sight of your dragon with the little girl warrior and her special sword swooping in is enough to make even the most dedicated soldier turn tail and run."

Linara tried to sit up, and didn't quite make it. "You let him go back into battle?" When last she'd seen Pax he'd been bloody, wounded, not at all as strong as he should be to fly and fight.

"We healed him," Juliet said. "Trust me; he is capable." She looked at her sisters, one and then the other. "How would one stop a dragon, if he was of a mind to fly away?"

Linara's eyes drifted shut. She was so tired!

"I thought I was dying," she whispered. "The dagger…"

"Stasio's dagger was fashioned to destroy a demon heart. You, my daughter, are much more than that."

"But…"

"Sleep, love," her mother's voice whispered. "You will be well, and your dragon-man will be well. Together you will…"

Isadora interrupted. "Don't tell everything! Good heavens, Sophie, leave the girl some secrets to discover for herself."

Secrets? There were still secrets? With that thought in her mind, Linara drifted off to sleep again. She dreamed of dragons.

CHAPTER 23

Pax landed on a patch of grass at the edge of the village. For the past few days he'd set down in this same spot so often the grass had been ripped to shreds by his talons; mud had been slung for a considerable distance. He'd accidentally knocked over one sapling with his tail, and Val had done her best to right the sad little tree. The sickly plant that leaned precariously to one side might survive. It might not.

The crooked limbs made an acceptable place to hang clothing. He didn't see anything wrong with his own nakedness, but others were alarmed. He shifted, then grabbed the red kilt from the crooked tree and wrapped it around his waist.

He was already tired of this war that was not his own, but he would not leave until Linara was well. Besides, he could not dismiss the joy he felt when he — with Val and Kitty riding upon his back — swooped in to take down a party of demons. There were fewer and fewer of them as days passed. Perhaps some hid. Others had somehow fought the evil inside themselves.

Still others, he had been told, had had the demonic half of themselves removed by a witch. Lyssa, they said her name was. She traveled with a skilled swordsman, her husband he had heard, and their children. Foolish demons had attempted to kidnap her, but they had not succeeded.

Could this witch help Linara?

Would the woman he loved still be Linara if a piece of herself was stripped away?

Linara did not have her mother's goodness, and she never would. The streaks of black in her aura were a part of her. It would be foolish to pretend to be someone she was not. He cared for all of her; he wanted all of her. Even the demon.

All his life he'd searched for a mate who was like him. A dragon. One who had been hatched, not born. And now...he wanted none but Linara. She was his mate. She was all that he needed.

As usual, Val didn't turn to face him until he'd had time to shift and cover himself. There had been a time when the child had asked him if he was "decent" before she'd turn around. The answer was always the same. No. He was not decent and never had been. Why pretend now?

As they walked toward the village, Val sighed in a girlish way. "I wish I could keep you."

Pax was horrified. "Keep me?"

"My own dragon! How stellar would that be?"

The horror intensified. "I am not a pet!"

Val made a girly, disgusted noise. "I know. But you must admit, we make a fine pair."

Kitty vibrated so strongly, Pax's ears hurt.

Val heard it, too. "Team, I mean. The three of us

make a fine team."

"Our task is a temporary one," Pax said. He was ready to leave, he wanted to leave, but he could not until things were settled with Linara. Would she come with him? Did she still love him?

"I guess you're not a pet," the girl said wistfully.

"No, I am not."

She sighed, spotted her father standing with a group of soldiers, and ran.

"Pet," Pax grumbled. And then he stopped.

There she was, awake and aware, standing outside the building that was still marked with her blood. Linara's heart had healed, thanks to her mother and her aunts.

She wore a clean, unstained dress. Of course she did. Her own frock had been sliced and bloodied beyond repair. This one was a pale yellow, and did not suit her as well as the blue had.

He cared not about what she wore. He'd thought she was dead. In all his years, he had never known such pain.

Linara turned her head and saw him standing there. She smiled, and waited. She waited for him.

This was a pain he did not need, the kind of pain he had never wanted. He could not protect her from the dangers of the world. No one could. What if next time she did die? What if there was no healer, no witch around to save her? Love meant loss, loss meant pain.

Since meeting Linara he had known a pleasure

greater than any other he had imagined, and yet he had also experienced that pain. Thanks to her his world had expanded, in ways that were both good and bad.

For a long moment, he stood there staring at her. He could fly away now, forget the war that was almost over, forget the woman who had the power to break his heart. He'd lived alone for a very long time, and he could live alone again.

Without companionship. Without love.

Without risk.

He continued walking, ignoring the greetings of those he passed, ignoring the stares and the whispers. No matter what happened, he was what he was. Shifter. Killer. Breather of fire. Dragon.

"You look well," Linara said. She was still weak, though she tried to hide that weakness from him.

He could tell her the same, lie and ignore the paleness of her face, the frailty of her bones. He did not.

"I love you," he said.

She smiled, and looked instantly stronger.

"I knew you'd come around."

He wrapped his arms around her. She was small and fragile, but there was a strength about her, even now. "Come with me," he whispered. "Return to the mountains with me. You will heal there. We will have everything we've ever wanted, just the two of us."

"I can't," she said.

And there it was, that agony he had known was coming, the pain of loving and losing.

"Not yet," she added, and the pain subsided. "Mama and Papa will leave tomorrow. My aunts and their husbands departed today."

"Because you are well," he said.

"Yes." She reached up and placed a hand on his cheek. "I need to find a way to tell them that I probably won't see them again. They might not take it well. Mama always wants her children and grandchildren close by. Family is important to her."

"And yet you will leave with me."

"You are my family now, Pax. I have told you many times, I love you."

He kissed her. He wanted much more than a kiss, but they were not alone. They might not be alone for days to come. He did not share her human need for privacy, but he did understand it.

When he drew away, he saw that there was more color in her cheeks, a new sparkle in her eyes. He fed her still.

He would feed her always.

Val was pleased to see that Cyrus stood near her father. He'd been hidden from her vantage point before, but as soon as she moved to the side...there he was.

Handsome, talented, more powerful than anyone had imagined he might be.

Since their arrival in the village, it had become clear that her friend and her father had come to a truce of sorts. They listened to one another. Neither bristled. It was an improvement, one for which she was grateful. She didn't want the two most important men in her life to be constantly at odds.

Perhaps she could not keep her dragon, but she would keep the wizard.

Cyrus said they'd marry one day, and she could see no reason to argue with him.

You will keep me, too, Kitty whispered.

I never imagined any other possibility.

"Valora," Cyrus said, nodding in her direction.

He always insisted on calling her by her full first name. She was never "Val" to him. Somehow that was all right with her. The name sounded kind of pretty when he said it.

The war would not be a long one. There were pockets of resistance, small groups of demons who had resisted Stasio's leadership but still fought for dominance. It would soon be over, and maybe then she could think about pretty things. Dresses and hair styles and hats. Well, no, no hats. Ewww. But maybe she'd learn to braid her hair, or at the least tame it. Somehow.

As she drew near, the others, even her father, departed. They had things to do, as did all soldiers. They nodded or waved to her as they hurried away. They acknowledged Cyrus, too. They respected him now. He shared valuable knowledge, about where the demons they needed to eliminate were located, and where some witch woman who could help had been living.

Cyrus was no longer a farmer's son. He was a seer. A wizard.

His eyes wandered to the couple standing on the other side of the village, and he nodded in that direction. "You like him."

"Pax? Of course, I like him." Duh. "He's a dragon. *A dragon.* He flies and breathes fire upon our enemies, and when we're in battle he protects me. Just this morning, he used his tail to…"

"Yes, yes, I know. He's a dragon."

"One of a kind, I suspect. Some men say he's the only one, that there won't be another like him, not ever."

Cyrus sighed, and his eyes kind of…flashed or twinkled or something. And then he said, "That's not true."

"There are others?" Val whispered. More dragons? Where? Were they friendly? Could they join in the war, as Pax had?

"Not yet," Cyrus answered, his voice as soft as hers. "Can you keep a secret?"

She hated secrets! Hated knowing anything she could not tell, hated keeping secrets from those she loved. Okay, from anyone she knew. And yet, she lifted her chin and answered, "Of course I can."

Cyrus placed a hand on her arm, and together they looked at the man who was the subject of their discussion. The man and his woman, who were so intensely focused on one another they had no idea they were being watched.

"The demon..."

"Linara," Val corrected. "Her name is Linara."

Again, Cyrus sighed. He did that a lot, these days. "Linara has much to discover about herself. She has incredible powers she's not yet discovered. She has...truly amazing capabilities."

He stopped speaking. *That* was the secret? That Linara was more powerful than she knew? No, there was more. There had to be.

Eventually, after several excruciating moments of silence, Cyrus continued. "She can become anything she wishes to be. Demon, human, witch, shifter. Dragon."

Val grabbed Cyrus' arm and held on tight. "Seriously? Linara can turn into a dragon like Pax?" How on earth was she going to keep this secret? How was she not going to tell someone? Anyone? Drat. As hard as it would be, she'd keep the secret. Because Cyrus had asked it of her.

"One day, she will. She has much to learn about herself before that happens, but..."

"And then she'll what...lay eggs? Make more dragons?"

Cyrus smiled. "She will not lay eggs."

"But you said..."

"He will."

EPILOGUE

The war was well behind them, as Linara and Pax again climbed a mountain, one she had not stepped upon before today, though her companion had been here at some point in the past. Summer had come and gone. Fall was fading. Soon there would be snow. And still, they traveled.

Not that their travels were unpleasant. Not at all. Their pace was a leisurely one. They made love often, and Pax fed her well. Some nights he flew and she watched. Other nights she rode upon his back, as Val once had. It was exhilarating. All of it! Flying, loving, moving toward a new life.

Now and then, they danced. By sunlight and moonlight, and by the light of the dragonstone they found here and there along the way, they danced.

On some days, especially if the terrain was difficult to traverse, they covered a great distance by air, but on other days they simply walked. There was pleasure in the journey itself.

Linara knew that dangers still existed in Columbyana, and always would, but she had no fears or doubts about moving on to a new life. Her family was safe, and Pax loved her. There was little else that mattered.

He seemed to move a bit faster than before, on this sunny and cold afternoon. They would soon reach the peak of this mountain, and judging by the history of their journey thus far they would head down and then back up again. Were these mountains endless?

He was there, at the peak, when he reached back and smiled at her. That smile always grabbed her heart. He offered his hand, and she took it. He gave a tug, and pulled her to his side.

Just feet away there was a sharp drop, but that's not where her eyes went. The land that spread below them was different from the mountains they'd traversed to get here. It was lushly green, even now. As far as she could see, there were rolling green hills. It looked as if the earth had been shaken out like a dusty rug and dropped into place, creases and crevices and all.

Here and there, ponds and lakes dotted the landscape with crystal clear blue waters. Well in the distance, massive, harsh mountains were already topped with snow.

"What is this place?" she asked, her voice low in awe.

"Home," Pax answered simply. "I have not been here for a very long time, but I wanted to share it with you."

He began to shift, and she backed away slowly. When the change was complete, she climbed upon his back and held on as he swooped across the lush blue and green lands. With the wind in her hair, she studied the landscape. The hills stretched as far as the eye could see. It was peaceful, beautiful, and as far as she could tell, completely uninhabited.

Was this where the dragon war had taken place, hundreds of years ago? Where man and beast had all but wiped one another from the face of the earth? She suspected yes, but it had been so long there was no sign of the violence that had taken place here. She sensed only peace, not war.

She loved riding on Pax's back, but suddenly she wished for the freedom of flight for herself. If she were a dragon, she could swoop over these hills whenever she felt the need. She could fly home on a whim to see her mother, her father, her siblings, and cousins. Juliet's home was not so far away, by air.

Nothing and no one was far away by air.

Pax would surely take her anywhere she wanted to go, but oh, the freedom of flight, the gift of fire…suddenly she longed for it. Surely a dragon would be a better mate for Pax than a half-demon woman. She wished…oh, she wished.

Her spine began to itch a little. She shrugged it off. Then her wrist burned a bit, and there was that itching again. She pushed her sleeve up and glanced at her wrist, and there it was.

A scale, as green as the trees she had been admiring and as tough as the mountains she had traversed, had appeared there, had grown there in a matter of seconds. She imagined the same was happening along her spine as she changed. As she became that which she wished to be. Was it possible? Was it possible that with a wish she could change so completely?

Yes, it was happening. Deep inside, she felt the change.

Linara leaned down and placed her head against Pax's neck.

You will never guess what's happening!

I do not need to guess. I feel it, too.

I did not know this was possible.

Neither did I.

He landed in a clearing near a pond that reminded her of the one which was now far away, where they had made love. Where he had learned that she'd planned to kill him and she'd found her Ksana power at last.

Pax took her hand in his and studied the wrist, kissing the single scale there before it faded away.

She gasped. "Where did it go? Was it a temporary thing? Oh, I wanted so much…"

Pax kissed her, probably to end her frantic rant. She did feel quite frantic.

When he pulled away, he said, "I love you, woman or dragon, demon or human. You are all of these things, and they are all mine. You are all mine."

"Now and forever."

He leaned down to rest his forehead against

hers. "I have so much to teach you."

She kissed him gently, reveling, as she always did, in the joy of his lips against hers. *Teach me to fly, love. Teach me to fly.*

LINDA WINSTEAD JONES

Linda's first book, the historical romance *Guardian Angel*, was released in 1994. In the years since she's written in several romance sub-genres under several names. In order of appearance, Linda Winstead; Linda Jones; Linda Winstead Jones; Linda Devlin; and Linda Fallon. She's a six time finalist for the RITA Award and a winner (for *Shades of Midnight*, writing as Linda Fallon) in the paranormal category. Most recently she's been involved in joint projects with Linda Howard, and has been rereleasing some of her backlist in ebook format. More information can be found at lindawinsteadjones.com, where you can sign up for her newsletter, at
www.facebook.com/LindaWinsteadJones
and on
www.facebook.com/LindaHowardLindaJones
and
Twitter @LWJbooks.